MELTED THE HEART OF A MENACE

P. WISE

URBAN AINT DEAD

CONTENTS

STAY CONNECTED!

Website: PrettiWise.com

   Instagram: @CEO.Pwise

   Facebook: Author P. Wise

   Facebook Business: Authoress P. Wise

   Facebook Group: Words of the Wise (P. Wise Book Group)

P.O Box 923
Brookhaven, PA 19015

SOUNDTRACKS

Scan the QR Code below to listen to the Soundtracks/Singles of some of your favorite U.A.D titles:

Don't have Spotify or Apple Music?
No Sweat!
Visit your choice streaming platform and search URBAN AINT DEAD.

Currently on lock serving a bid?
JPay, iHeartRadio, WHATEVER!
We got you covered.

Simply log into your facility's kiosk or tablet, go to music and
search URBAN AINT DEAD.

URBAN AINT DEAD

SUBMISSIONS

Submit the first three chapters of your completed manuscript to <u>urbanaintdead@gmail.com</u>, subject line: Your book's title. The manuscript must be in a .doc file and sent as an attachment. The document should be in Times New Roman, double-spaced, and in size 12 font. Also, provide your synopsis and full contact information. If sending multiple submissions, they must each be in a separate email. Have a story but no way to submit it electronically? You can still submit to URBAN AINT DEAD. Send in the first three chapters, written or typed, of your completed manuscript to:

URBAN AINT DEAD
P.O Box 448
Maybrook, NY 12543

DO NOT send original manuscript. Must be a duplicate.
Provide your synopsis and a cover letter containing your full
contact information.
Thanks for considering URBAN AINT DEAD.

DEDICATION

This is dedicated to everyone out there that's blocking their blessing from gaining a real man or woman in their life. Don't allow your past experiences to hinder your future happiness. Life's too short.

Happy Holidays my WISE Queens & Kings.
-P. Wise

TREASURE "TINK" KING

"Lay still, damnit," I snapped at my best friend Maleah.

I was doing her recovery massage. We had just gotten back from Miami a week before, where she got her BBL done.

"It hurts like hell, Tink," she cried, calling me by my nickname. Tears were literally making their escape from her eyes.

"I told you this wasn't going to be no easy shit," I reminded her.

When it came to having cosmetic surgery, the actual procedure was the easy part; the recovery was what needed to be worried about. Everyone's pain tolerance was different so, when getting the massages, I always got different reactions.

"I know, Tink, damn," she snapped at me out of anger.

She was acting like I placed a gun to her head and told her to go and get her body done. Once she saw I got mine done and I had no complaints, she wanted to go ahead and give it a shot.

Maleah was my childhood best friend. We both grew up on the same block in Bed-Stuy, Brooklyn and attended the same school from grade level all the way to high school. She was my right-hand and been a loyal friend since day one. Out of our crew that consisted of four of us, she was my main bitch.

"One more roll and we're finished. Let's just get it over with," I tried to persuade her.

She squeezed her eyes shut tightly and took a deep breath in and out. "Okay, go ahead."

I went on and quickly finished her session, so she could get out my massage room with her cry baby self.

After I experienced getting my body done, I saw the importance of recovery and post operation. I went to school, studied therapeutics massage and beauty and became a licensed massage therapist and esthetician. After taking on a few clients and gaining more experience, I landed a job at Body Right LLC in Brooklyn where I worked for the past three years.

Body Right LLC was where all the ladies came after going through cosmetic surgery to get their recovery massages and more. Plus, it was a comforting place to many when it came to all their massage, body care, and relaxing needs.

"Whew, thank God, it's over," Maleah exclaimed, looking relieved.

"Girl." I side-eyed her and curled my lip up. She was so extra when she wanted to be.

"So, how are things with Justin?" she pried, referring to my boyfriend of two years.

Justin Jenkins was my on and off-again boyfriend. We lived together, but it didn't feel like it at times. He would stay out all night and, sometimes, even days would past and he wouldn't make it home. His excuse was he was on the road jugging and making money for us. I knew what I had signed up for two years prior when we got together. The nice threads, date and club nights were lit in my eyes. That was before I really understood what I needed in a man. At the time we met, I was dealing with trying to balance life and my mother dying from cancer.

Justin was an outlet and was helping out with a lot when it came to my bills and my mother's medical expenses. While he kept me satisfied financially in some sort of way, I yearned for more of his time, especially since I knew he was out in the streets fuckin' on hoes.

"Things are cool. Can't complain," I simply put. Even though Maleah was my girl, I just knew better than to speak too much on my personal business.

As soon as I was finished with her, I attended to my other client who was prepped and waiting for me. My client had already passed the beginning stages of healing, so her session went by quick; I was literally in and out.

When I left out the room to head to the front by the waiting area, I saw my boss, Sarena, smelling a bouquet of roses at the front desk.

"Awwwhhh, that's so sweet," I sang. "Who's it from?"

"Oh, this dude I just started talking to; he's a sweetheart with deep pockets," she stated while smiling at the roses.

"Oh yeah? You can never go wrong with one of those."

"At all, he's even talking about helping me expand the business."

Hearing her say those words got me upset a bit. It wasn't anything towards her, it was towards Justin. For the longest time, he kept promising me that he was going to help me open my own spa and recovery home. Time and time again as I tried my best to save up and start the process, he would come up with excuses; it was discouraging as fuck.

"Good for you." I smiled.

Moments later, Maleah walked to the waiting area dressed and ready to go. "Alright, bye friend. I'll see you tomorrow for Thanksgiving, right?"

Shit, I forgot, I thought.

"Yup, sure will," I confirmed because I had no other choice.

We hugged one another goodbye, and I returned to work.

THANKSGIVING DAY

"Hands on your knees (ho), hands on your knees (ow). Shake that ass for Drake (yup), now, shake that ass for me," Sexyy Red rapped her verse on *Rich Baby Daddy* by Drake, featuring her and SZA.

The girls and I were shaking our ass and having a time after we filled our bellies with everything a person could imagine having for Thanksgiving. Despite getting into it with Justin earlier that day about us not spending time for the holiday knowing it was a hard one for me, I tried to enjoy myself. My girls knew how to get me out of a funky ass mood, which was why I appreciated them a lot.

A year before, I spent Thanksgiving with my mother and Justin. It was just us three at home, munching and laughing. That Thanksgiving was the last one I would ever spent with my moms. She passed the following month on Christmas day.

The holidays used to be the most exciting time in my life but, after losing her, it just didn't feel right celebrating without her. My girls were aware of everything, hence the reason they tried to keep me active and happy. Justin, on the other hand, felt making money was more important than spending time with me on a day like that.

"Alright y'all, I'm finna dip. I'm tired than a mudda," I joked in a Jamaican accent.

"How you gon' get home? Let me drive you," Maleah offered.

"No, stay and have fun. I'll take an Uber."

"You sure?"

"Yes, I'm positive, girl."

I grabbed my phone and requested a ride and, just my luck, one accepted and was only three minutes away. Gathering my belongings, I slipped into my winter coat and grabbed my things. Quickly saying my goodbyes to the girls, I made my way downstairs to meet my ride.

As soon as I reached the front stoop, he pulled up. Before walking up to the car, I matched the license plates from the one on the app to his car. Too much bullshit was happening in the world not to take proper precaution.

I slid into the backseat and got comfortable, as the driver pulled off toward my place. Scrolling through my social medias, I looked at all the happy couples that were out enjoying each other and couldn't help but feel a sting of jealousy. I just didn't know what it was gon' take for Justin to act right.

Quickly, I went deep into my thoughts about him and our relationship, thinking about how things were in the beginning and how they had changed. I analyzed my actions and what I could've done to better the situation, but I damn near came up empty on suggestions.

Bang!

Off the huge impact, my body was tossed to the other side of the backseat as my head smashed against the window. My vision became blurred, but I still had some kind of consciousness. I reached for my bag to get my phone but a wave of pain hit me, causing me to faint back onto the seat.

I heard voices near the car and instantly felt some relief to know we were going to be saved. The driver wasn't moving, nor did he say a word, so I knew he was knocked out unconscious or, worst, dead.

Someone was tugging at the doors and finally pried them open. Still with a blurred vision, I tried to see, but it was still hard.

"Aye, it's a joint in here," I heard a guy say.

"Damn, he was on a ride," another one stated. "Fuck it, we gotta grab her too."

Huh, what? I thought.

As soon as I felt hands grabbing on me and pulling me out of the vehicle, panic set in. I had no clue what the hell was going on, so the first thing that came to mind was to kick and scream.

"Stop, please, stop! Get off me!" I pleaded, as they got me out of the car and over one of their shoulders.

Hollering at the top of my lungs, I was shoved in the back of a trunk with nothing but a fearful feeling. Immediately after, someone else was pushed into the trunk beside me, which I assumed was the driver. The door was slammed closed.

"Help, please, help!" I screamed as I kicked at the door with all my might. My body was in so much pain but, at that moment, I didn't care.

We drove some ways and, after a while, when I saw I was hollering for no reason, I just stopped and cried to myself. The person next to me was still out and hadn't moved an inch.

When we finally stopped, I heard doors opening and closing, then footsteps coming and stopping at the trunk. I felt around for anything I could've used to hit them with, but the trunk was completely empty. Once the door opened, almost immediately, they placed something over my head and I saw nothing but darkness, followed by tape being stuck over my mouth.

Lifted out the trunk and over someone's shoulder, I gave a hard time once again. But my little frame was no match for the brolic ass man that was carrying me.

"Chill the fuck out, yo," he growled.

Hearing the tone of his voice and him squeezing my thigh hard made me keep quiet, for the moment that was.

We entered what I assumed was a building of some kind because I no longer felt the biting cold winds. He carried me down some steps and down a hall. Placing me down on a cold concrete floor, I heard him quickly shuffle out of the room and close the door.

I snatched the bag off my head since they never bounded my hands and took a look around. My vision still wasn't a hundred percent clear, but it was better. The Uber driver was lying next to me motionless and still. When I didn't hear anyone outside of the room door, I went ahead and tried to wake him up.

"Hey, hey, are you okay?" I asked as I gave his body a couple of nudges. After I saw he wasn't responding, I checked his pulse to see if he was alive or dead, but he was still breathing, thankfully.

I heard footsteps coming my way, and the door flung open with a few guys wearing skully masks. They rushed in and separated the driver and me, dragging us on opposite sides of the room.

"What's this about? Please, let me go," I pleaded.

Two guys carried a large bucket of water and stepped in front of the driver. Seconds later, they poured the water down on him, causing him to jump out of his unconsciousness.

"What the fuck?" he asked, trying to catch his breath and bearings.

Looking around the room, he noticed we were in some deep shit. His eyes roamed from the guys and then to me. While most of the men were inside of the room with us, one stood by the door in a calm manner. I continued to watch him from the corner of my eyes, but I noticed he kept his attention on me.

"Where that package you were supposed to drop off two days ago?" one of the guys bent down to his eye level and asked.

"What, what package?" the driver stuttered.

The guy hung his head and grabbed the gun from his waistline. "Where the fuck is the package, David Rice?" he asked again, that time calling his government name; I remembered seeing his name on the Uber app.

"Fuck," David whispered to himself but loud enough for everyone to hear. "I so-so-sold it."

"Nigga, you sold five bricks? Aye Tee, I think you need to get his ass on the team," the guy joked as he spoke to the one standing in the doorway. "Where the fuck the money at then?"

"I'll tell you, just please don't kill me," David bargained.

"Man, where the shit at?"

"It's at my place, under my bed," he informed them.

The guy turned and looked at the other one by the door, who then gave him a head nod, prompting him to move away from David. Within that very second, he stood to the side, and a bullet was lodged in the center of David's head; I almost lost my shit. My body shook vigorously as my whole life flashed before me.

"What we doing with her?" he asked the guy, who lowered his gun and started to walk away.

He turned around and looked at me for a moment. "Off her," he stated in a nonchalant tone.

"Nooo!" I shouted with tears in my eyes. "Please don't. I won't say anything. I don't even know how y'all look."

They all just stood there looking at me beg for my life, and I didn't give a fuck how I looked. Snotty nose and all, they were going to feel me. The quiet one, which I assumed to be the boss since he was calling the shots, walked over to me and squatted down.

"How I know you not just saying anything to get up outta here?" he asked.

"You don't know that, but I pray you give me a chance. I promise, this never happened."

"Chances get you killed and, in my case, could get us locked the fuck up."

"That won't happen because I don't know shit."

I searched his eyes for any sign of humanity while I noticed him searching mine for what I believed was to see if I was being truthful, which I was. "Please, I don't wanna die like this," I cried.

"So, how do you want to die?" He continued to stare at me without blinking.

"I don't know but not anytime soon."

"Man, let her go, Tee. We'll just keep an eye on her," the shooter spoke.

"Where her shit at?" Tee asked, remembering his name.

One guy grabbed my bag that was in the room's corner and handed it to Tee. He started to looking through it and found my wallet with my ID card and work badge.

"Treasure Issa Naami King. What a long fuckin' name," he ridiculed, chuckling afterwards. Taking pictures of them, he slipped the contents back into my wallet and placed it back inside my bag.

"Listen, Treasure, as you know, I can kill you right now. But because I feel a little generous and my boy suggested I let you go, I'll do so. But I will be watching you and, if you even think about opening up your mouth, I will make sure you die slowly just because you didn't keep your word. We got an understanding?"

I nodded my head quickly as I felt myself choking up.

"Words, Treasure, I need to hear you say it."

"We have an understanding. You have my word," I confirmed.

"Good girl."

He stood up and walked out of the room, never looking

back. The same bag that was on my head when I was carried in was back covering my vision as I felt them pick me up off the ground. That time around, there was no kicking and screaming, but I still felt angst knowing they could've easily changed their minds.

I was placed in the backseat of a vehicle different from my arrival, but I had no complaints. My mouth was shut but my mind was racing a thousand miles per hour while I prayed I made it home safely.

A few days had passed since the whole ordeal. My body was hurting from the accident and my mind had been playing tricks on me. Any time I closed my eyes, I saw David slumped against the wall with a bullet in his head. After the smoked cleared, someone trained the gun on me and, any time I heard a shot being fired, I would jump out of my sleep.

Monday rolled around faster than I could think. I had a few days to stay in the bed and try to get myself together. Justin wasn't home all weekend, which for once I was actually happy about that. I didn't have to explain why I came home so late after Friendsgiving with the girls or why I was bruised up and startled by every little noise I heard.

Knowing I had to act normal and like nothing happened, I rolled out of my bed and got dressed to head into work. I knew it would've taken some time for me to get my mind off things and, while doing so, I had to keep a straight face.

When I arrived at work, I went about my day as usual. I

took clients and walk-ins just to keep myself distracted from drowning in my thoughts. Anytime I went outside for a little fresh air, I felt like someone was watching me. They said they were going to keep eyes on me, but I didn't think they were literally going to do so. But understanding the severity of the crime, I might've done the same.

"Tink!" I heard my boss yell out to me.

I was in my room just chilling before my next client came. I had a good hour before the appointment. "Yeah, I'm coming!" I hollered back as I left out the room and made my way to the front.

A fine, light skinned guy was standing at the receptionist's desk. From what I could see, he had tattoos all on his neck and the side of his head. He wore a low cut but had a Fendi winter hat on. His threads were expensive and he looked to be about six feet in height, which was tall to me since I stood at only five-two.

"This gentleman would like to get a full body massage. Can you take him before your four o'clock?" Serena asked.

I wasn't doing shit but scrolling on social media, and a distraction was what I needed. When I looked at him closer, he looked familiar, but I couldn't put my finger on where I knew him from.

"Sure, come with me." I motioned for him to follow me to the back.

When we got in the room, I gave him instructions to take off his clothes, except for his boxers, and lie on the bed. Then, I instructed him to cover his lower half with the towel I provided him with. I couldn't help but to scan his body as it was tatted from every angle possible. His entire chest, stomach, back, and arms, even his right leg, was riddled with art work.

I dimmed the lights and turned on the music softly to get the vibe going. My clients being comfortable while I worked on them was important. I wanted to take them to another place while they were in my care. Starting his massage, I oiled his skin down nicely. My hand passed on his back, feeling a huge scar that lined from the top to the side of his stomach. Looking at the mark reminded me of a situation that happened to someone I knew as a kid. He was sliced in that same spot; I remembered it like it had just been the day prior.

Shaking my thoughts, I continued to massage his body from head to toe. When he came in, he was tense but, by the time I was finished with him, he was relaxed. I had that effect on everyone that I touched.

"I'll step out, so you can get dressed," I told him as I exited out the door.

To kill a few minutes, I went and used the bathroom, then made my rounds to check on my co-workers on my way back to my room. When I got back, I knocked on the door and waited to hear a response before walking in.

"Yo," I heard him say.

I walked in, and he was putting on his Cuban link around his neck. Since we were finally up close and he didn't have anything blocking me from seeing all of him, I noticed who it was.

"Treyce?" I asked.

He looked up at me with a blank look. "It's Trigg now," he corrected.

What I thought was a reunion quickly turned into a terrifying moment. I connected the voice, eyes, and body structure; it was the Tee guy from Thanksgiving night, someone I knew as Treyce.

TREYCE "TRIGG" TAYLOR

The moment I saw Tink in the basement of my trap house, I couldn't believe my eyes. It had been years since I saw her at the home her moms used to work at. When I went through her stuff and found her ID, it only confirmed it was her ass for real.

Tink's moms, Ms. King, was the manager of the home I was placed in as a youth. I grew up in the foster system since the age of seven after they murdered my moms right in front of me. She had a dope boy for a boyfriend and, when they couldn't get to him, they got to someone close to his heart. That day turned me cold, and I was never the same.

"Wh-what are you doing here?" Tink asked in a hushed tone. Tears were forming in her eyes, as I noticed her body shook. I knew I scared her, and that's exactly how I wanted her to feel.

I knew Tink since we were kids around the age of eleven, but a lot of time passed and people changed. I didn't give a fuck if she was blood related; I would've gone about the situation the same. My freedom and life were important, and no one was going to threaten that. I had to see where her head was at.

"Just thought I'd swing past and check in on you, that's all." I smirked.

"I told you I would not say shit."

I sized her up and down and took a step closer, invading her space. "Shorty, I don't give a fuck about none of that. I'll be around to make sure you don't say shit."

"Wow, shorty? You're definitely not the Treyce I know."

"That's the thing, I ain't Treyce. My name is Trigg."

I took a big risk approaching her the way I did. She became aware of my true identity, but I didn't give a fuck. It was imperative she knew I was not someone to play with, and what better way than to pull up on her myself?

"What happened to you?" she asked in a soft tone.

Everything happened, I thought.

"A lot, but that's neither here nor there. I just came to test your temperature, ma. I'll see you around." I grabbed my jacket and left out the room, leaving her standing there looking lost and scared.

On my way out, I tossed a couple of bills on the receptionist's desk. "The rest is her tip," I informed the person and walked out the front door.

Hopping in the passenger side of my whip, my boy, Wave, pulled off as soon as I closed the door.

"The fuck took you so long, nigga?" he queried.

"A nigga got a massage, fuck you mean?" I retorted.

He bussed out laughing hysterically, then looked over at me. Wave was my right-hand man, probably the only person I trusted to a certain extent, which was surprising because I didn't even trust myself fully. We had hit it off when we were both locked up on Rikers Island. He showed his loyalty and, when we touched back down on the streets, he never left my side.

"So, you went in there to do one thing and ended up getting rubbed on while I sat out here in the cold?"

"Son, you was not in the cold; this muthafucker hot as hell in here."

"Yeah, aight nigga, you grimy as fuck for that." He bent the block hard as hell.

"And I made her give me a massage," I added.

"Nah, my nigga, you a wild boy. She know who you are?"

"Yeah, but I ain't worried. Shorty ain't a dumb broad."

"You talking like you know for sure." He looked at me as we stopped at a red light.

"Because I do."

The Tink I knew was solid. When me and the other boys at the home used to do wild shit, Tink never told. She used to cover for us on many occasions without us even having to ask. She was one of those ride or die chicks. People grew older and changed, but traits like that usually stayed embedded in them.

"Aight, son, you the boss anyway," Wave spoke and lifted his hands up in surrender.

We pulled up to one of my trap houses where most of the scamming was done. I had a whole set up where some of my niggas handled the drug side of things while the other half ran the scamming business. A nigga like me felt like I had to have my hands in everything, different streams of income. I even killed niggas for a living and sometimes ran down on them too, whatever made my bag bigger.

"Tell Manny to give you the two bags that's for the bump man," I told Wave. He nodded and jumped out of the vee and ran into the house.

When the day was over, it was usually a ton of shit my guys went out to the stores and swiped. It would be name brand clothes, sneakers, phones, laptops, iPads, and a bunch of other shit. And since it was Black Friday, a few days before and cyber-Monday, they raked in all kinds of shit to sell.

We never resold shit ourselves. It was different bump men I had in my pocket, which were people, mostly jew niggas, who would buy the shit off us and resell themselves. I never had to get rid of things piece by piece; it would take forever and I didn't have that kind of time. Since it was the holidays, the bump men were always looking for things. It was the busiest and most lucrative time of the year.

Wave came back out of the spot with two huge duffle bags in each hand. I popped the trunk for him to put them inside; then, he returned behind the wheel.

"Going to the bump now?" he asked.

I had my head down in my phone because a text message

had just came in from this little joint I was fuckin' around with.

China: Pussy wet and food on the table, you coming or nah?

Me: On the wayyyy...

"Nah, I'm finna go link with shorty real quick," I informed him. "Drive yourself to your whip and I'll take myself."

Wave did what I told him and, before we knew it, we were going our separate ways. I had him hold on to the bags that were in the trunk since I knew he was going to get to his crib before I got to mine.

About twenty minutes later, I pulled up to China's spot in Queens, parked, and made my way to her front door. From the moment I stepped onto her stoop, the aroma of food hit my nostrils. I felt my stomach grumble, not noticing I had gone all day without eating.

I knocked on the door and, seconds later, it swung open with China standing there in just a bra and thong. She turned and walked away without even saying shit to me but motioned for me to follow her to the dining room. My plate was already on the table, along with a drink. I sat and dug right in, not paying her a lick of attention.

"Baby, why didn't you come over for Thanksgiving?" she sat across from me and asked.

"Because I ain't into all that shit. Plus, a nigga was busy handling business," I told her between chewing.

I was occupied like a muthafucker that night and, while I should've used her as an alibi, I said fuck it and went about my way.

"And what I told you about calling me that shit?" I added.

"I don't get you. You come here fucking me good, eating here, sleeping whenever you want to, and spending money on me, but I can't call you baby?"

I continued to eat and not pay her any mind. The way she was acting was the very reason I didn't like to fuck with a bitch after a certain period. They caught feelings and thought all types of shit in their heads. I ain't had no time for whatever it was she was hooting and hollering about.

"Trigg, you don't hear me talking to you?" she pushed.

"Nah, I don't. But I do want my dick sucked." I leaned back in my seat, then looked between her and my lap.

China rolled her eyes but walked over to me, dropped to her knees, and undid my jeans. Within seconds, she shoved my whole dick in her mouth and got him awoke with her warm, wet mouth. That night, I fucked her until she stopped nagging and threw her some money. I knew it was only going to shut her up for a little while, but it was good enough for me.

The following morning, I found myself in China's bed still but well rested. My phone was vibrating over and over again. When I reached and grabbed it, I saw Wave's name on the screen.

"Yo, son," I answered.

"Twelve at the spa talking to shorty," he revealed.

Fuckkk!

TINK

"I told you for the hundredth time. I got in the car, then ended up getting out because my friend took me home," I lied.

Two detectives came to the spa and questioned me about the night of David's disappearance. In the back of my head, I figured they'd come looking for me, but I prayed day in and day out they didn't. I guess God didn't hear my prayer.

"Ms. King, is there any way we can call this friend of yours to confirm your story?" the woman detective asked.

Fuck, I knew this was coming, I said to myself. *Think Tink, think.*

"Uh, yeah, sure. Her name is Maleah," I blurted out.

"And does this Maleah have a number?"

I rattled out Maleah's number quickly, hoping they mixed up the numbers. Although I wanted to give the wrong number on purpose, I knew better than to intentionally fuck that up.

"Alright, we'll be in contact if there's anything else we need. Thank you for your time," she spoke and left out my room with her partner close behind.

The moment I knew they were out of the spa, I got on my phone and called Maleah to give her a heads up.

"Hey, baby, wassup?" she answered.

"If a detective call you and asks you anything, just let them know you took me home the night of Thanksgiving. Say I was in an Uber, but you were on your way out and took me home instead, okay?" I spoke quickly.

"Huh? What the hell going on Tink?"

"I'll explain later, but I just need you to stick to that story, aight?"

"I got you," she assured me.

"Thanks, I'll talk to you later. Love you."

"Love you, too."

I let out a huge breath, one that I didn't notice I was holding in the entire time the detectives were in my presence. Not even a good minute had passed after I hung up and my door was opening with Serena poking her head inside.

"You okay, mama?" she pried.

Serena knew good and well she didn't give a fuck if I was alright or not; she just wanted to see what the hell was going on, but I knew better.

"Yes, I'm fine." I shot her a fake smile.

"I'm here if you want to talk about whatever it is."

I bet, I told myself as I eyed her.

Thankfully, she caught my drift and left out, closing the door behind her. I sat back in my chair and just started to take deep breaths in and out. It was no doubt my pressure was high at that moment. My anxiety was through the roof as well, and it wasn't because of the detectives but because of what Trigg would do to me if he even thought I was running my mouth.

"Treasure, your ten o'clock is here," I heard the receptionist Crystal announce from the other side of the door.

"Okay, I'll be right out," I told her. Gathering my thoughts and emotions, I got myself together and went to get my client.

The rest of the day was tense but mostly in my mind. I kept busy, doing any and everything to keep my mind off of things, but it was indeed a challenge. When my last client left, I cleaned up and dashed out the door without an ounce of delay. Besides the cold weather, I wanted to hurry and get home before it got too late. I would usually hop in an Uber or Lyft, but those apps were deleted off my phone; I wanted no parts at all. So, I had no other choice but to get my boujee ass on the train.

Just when I was about to walk down the steps to the subway, I heard a car beep their horn twice. Looking up, I saw a snow-white Benz pulling up and the window started to roll down. When I saw Trigg's face, my heart dropped instantly.

"Get in," he demanded.

My feet felt like a ton of bricks was holding them down. Not a muscle in my body was trying to move.

"I ain't gon' tell you again. Get the fuck in the car before I drag yo ass in here myself," he grilled.

Out of nowhere, my feet felt light as feathers and were moving toward his car. Before I knew it, I was inside, sitting in his passenger seat with him pulling off.

For a good while, he didn't say a word as he maneuvered throughout the streets of Brooklyn. My eyes bounced between him and the road to pay attention to where he was going and what he was doing. Between my heart racing and my palms sweating, I wasn't sure what to think. I just knew I was fucked.

"Where are we going?" I mustered up the courage to ask.

He didn't respond right away. "That depends on what kind of conversation you had with twelve," he finally spoke.

"It wasn't anything major."

"I'll be the judge of that. What did they ask and what you told them?"

I gave him the rundown of our conversation, which was relatively short, not leaving out the part that I needed to insert Maleah into things. Everything I told him was the truth. I had just prayed he believed me.

"So, that's everything? You're not leaving anything out?"

I saw him watch me out of the corner of his eyes. "That's everything, word to my mother. May she rest in peace," I assured him.

Trigg swerved out of traffic and pulled over abruptly. "Wait, Mama King dead?" he asked with much disbelief in his voice.

"Yeah." I put my head down.

"Fuckkk."

Trigg had formed a close bond with my mother during his stay at the home. While the workers gave him a hard time, my mother always had a soft spot for him. But not too soft because she didn't allow me to hang around him.

Silence filled the car, and all that was heard was the traffic moving past us. We were both deep in our thoughts; Trigg processing the news and me just simply thinking about my queen that I missed dearly.

After a while of us just sitting there, he finally placed the car back in drive and pulled off. A few minutes back onto the road, I noticed we were heading to my place. At that point, I didn't even ask how he knew where I lived. I figured he remembered from my ID or him having eyes on me.

A sense of relief came over me, so I sat back in the passenger seat in silence. Trigg wasn't much of a talker since we were kids, and I noticed he grew up in the same ways. He was one of those get to the point kind of people and never had the energy to beat around the bush. I respected it but, sometimes, it was threatening.

As we pulled up to my place, I saw Justin walking up towards our building. It looked like he had just parked his car and got out because he was carrying bags. Justin was gone since Thanksgiving and finally came home from what he claimed to had been a business trip. I wish I could've said I was happy to see him, but I wasn't.

I opened the door but, before getting out of the car, I looked over at Trigg, who was looking out the window. "Ummm, thank you, I guess," I blurted out.

He didn't respond or even look my way. All I could've thought of was how rude and ignorant he was.

Continuing out of the car, I closed the door and walked up to the building. Justin was facing in my direction, so he saw me exiting out Trigg's Benz. By the look on his face, he had already assumed the worst.

"Who the fuck is that?" Justin asked while watching Trigg pull off quickly down the street.

"Just an old friend," I simply answered and walked past him into the building. I felt him stare a hole through my back the entire way upstairs.

When we made it into our apartment, I rushed straight to the room to get undressed and hop in the shower. While washing my skin, I heard Justin shuffling through things, making loud noises. He had kid tendences when he was upset about something and, clearly, he was throwing a tantrum.

Stepping out of the shower, I dried my skin and went into the bedroom. Justin was sitting on his side of the bed with his head buried in his phone. But once he saw I was back in the room, he dropped his phone on the bed and just stared at me.

"So, you not gon' tell me who the fuck that was?" he asked in an aggressive tone.

"I already told you. It's nothing more to tell, Justin," I answered.

"Tink, I ain't stupid. That was a whole nigga in that car."

He assumed it was a nigga in the car. Trigg's Benz was blacked out completely. It was even hard to see out from the inside, so I knew he was cappin' and just fishing.

"Justin, please don't start. You left me hanging for a week, missed Thanksgiving and all. So, don't come up in here wild'n and shit."

I threw my t-shirt over my head and got in the bed. He was just standing there looking at me like he wanted to do something.

"Fuck this shit, I'm out." He went into the closet and started throwing clothes in a bag.

"Where are you going?" I quizzed.

"I need to go cool off. I'll be gone for a few days." He grabbed the bag, his phone, and left out the room. A few moments later, I heard the apartment door open and shut.

There I was about to spend another night in bed alone when I was supposed to be sharing it with him. It was becoming overbearing mentally, emotionally, and physically. I hadn't had sex with Justin in a while and I had needs; my toys were holding me down, but I needed the real thing.

Fuck it, fuck him, I thought as I got comfortable and tucked myself in.

"Tink, hurry the hell up, man," Maleah fussed over the phone.

I didn't know why I even answered it, knowing she was going to talk her shit like it was going to make me move any faster. We were about to head to the club for the night; it was well needed.

Looking myself over once more in the mirror, I was content with my fit. I grabbed my things and hurried out the door before I heard the horn blowing. As soon as I got in the car, she peeled off before I could shut the door.

"Take my fuckin' foot off, will you? The fuck!" I snapped.

"You still have it though, right?" she sassed back.

Maleah turned up the music and made her way through the gritty cold streets of Brooklyn. Our destination for the night was Starlets for one of the hottest party of the year.

It took us about thirty minutes to get to the club and, when we got there, it had just hit one o'clock a.m. The line was long as hell. People were outside damn near having a party on the streets. It was a circus.

Maleah had the connection to one of the party promoters at the club, so we had reserved parking and didn't have to wait on the line to get inside. When we stepped foot in the club, it was a zoo. The vibe was lit as hell, and the place was packed. We were ushered to a section where a bunch of niggas had nothing but bad bitches surrounding them, as they threw money and popped bottles.

We got situated in a spot and joined in on the fun. They gave us our own bottles of Belaire and ones to throw, so digging in our own pockets was out of the question. I took a swig of my bottle and got in tune with what was going on around me.

About an hour later, I was feeling nice and tipsy after finishing a bottle and on to the second one, that time Rose.

"Bitch, I needed this, thank you!" I yelled above the music to Maleah.

My dude was always gone, I was sexually frustrated, I got kidnapped and almost killed, and work had been kicking my ass. That night, I said fuck everything and let loose, making sure to enjoy myself. That was until I spotted Justin.

For a minute, I thought my eyes were playing tricks on me since I had a lot to drink but, when I focused in, I realized they weren't. Justin was in the club with my boss, Serena.

What the fuck? I thought.

"What's wrong?" Maleah asked as she noticed a change in my demeanor.

Before she could ask another question, I threw my bag around my body, poured out the rest of the liquor, held onto the bottle tightly and swiftly made my way to where they were. I heard Maleah yelling behind me, but it didn't stop me.

When I reached them, their backs were turned to me, so they had no idea I was coming. I cocked the bottle back and bashed it onto Serena's head. The bottle didn't break, so I quickly swung and smashed it upside Justin's head before he even knew what was going on.

Immediately, I felt hands on me, grabbing my body away. Out of nowhere, I saw Maleah fly into action, grabbing Serena by the hair and pouncing on her.

"Let me the fuck go!" I yelled as I kicked. I had a flashback of the night they snatched me when I was kicking and screaming for dear life.

Maleah was snatched off of Serena and being carried right behind me on our way out of the club. Before reaching outside, I saw a face I was surprised to see, especially there at that moment.

Really, what the fuck?

TRIGG

"Aye man, let her go," I demanded of the security.

Walking into Starlets, I saw the bouncer carrying Tink out in an aggressive manner. First thing that came to mind was getting him to let her go, then find out what the fuck was going on.

With no questions, he put her down. The owner, Tanz, who was standing beside me, was one of my boys and someone who pushed my products for me in his club. That night, I pulled up to drop off some shit for him and peeped the scene.

"Fuck is going on?" I asked.

"She just bashed two people in their heads with a bottle," he revealed.

Oh shit, I thought. I looked at Tink, who had a mean scowl on her face, looking like she was still on go.

"Aight, we got them," my boy Tanz told the bouncers, prompting them to walk off back inside the club.

"How y'all got here?" I asked Tink.

She looked at me, rolled her eyes, and stormed out the door with her friend behind her. I took a deep breath because I knew if she continued to give all that attitude, I was going to have her hemmed up somewhere by her neck. Part of me didn't give a fuck about what happened but, since I inserted myself, I had to finish what I started.

Following them outside, I grabbed her arm and turned her to face me. "Didn't I ask yo ass a question?" I snapped.

"And I don't have to answer it. Leave me the fuck alone." She snatched her arm back.

People started to look at us and I hated that kind of attention, but it was too late; I was already in my bag. I grabbed her ass again and dragged her towards my whip. Her friend was in the back cussing and hollering like she lost her mind.

"What the fuck is wrong with you? Let her go!" she shouted.

"Mind yo fuckin' business," I turned and grilled, shooting her a menacing stare.

She quickly stopped in her tracks and stood there, watching as I continued to drag Tink's ass to my car. Tanz came back outside to see what was going on.

"Aye bro, make sure she get home," I told him, referring to her friend.

"I don't need no one to do shit. I drove." She dangled her keys in the air. "Tink, you good?"

Tink looked at me and, while she was hesitant at first, I shot her a look. She looked at her friend and nodded her head. As her homegirl walked away, I opened the car door for Tink.

"Get in," I demanded. She sat her ass inside, folding her arms and poking out her lips. I rounded the car and hopped in behind the wheel, started it up, and pulled out of the parking lot.

While driving, I kept glimpsing over at her and saw she had tears rolling down her face. It took me aback because I wasn't sure what transpired inside the club for her to be so emotional.

"You good?" I lowered the music and asked.

She started to sniffle and wipe away her tears. "I'm good," she simply answered.

"Clearly, you're not because you're crying and in your feelings."

"Nah, I'm just upset I didn't kill them."

Shit, maybe she is about that life after all, I thought.

"I hear you, Ms. Colombiana."

She grilled me through the corner of her eyes but it didn't move me, not one bit; it was kind of cute though. After the whole ordeal, she still looked intact. Her hair was in place, makeup looked nice, and her fit had a nigga eyeing her. Tink was always a good-looking girl but, as a woman, she was gorgeous. Any nigga could've seen her beauty miles away.

By the time I reached her place and parked, she stopped crying and was just resting her head on the window.

"You good to go?" I quizzed. I could tell she was tipsy and just wanted to make sure she could've gotten upstairs safely.

"Yeah, I am," she said lowly.

Tink opened the door and, when she tried to stand up, she damn near broke an ankle, causing her to land right back inside the car. Looking over at her, I just shook my head. The car was already parked, so I got out and went to help her. I secured the doors and guided her to the building. She got the keys out of her bag and handed it to me to open the door. We made our way upstairs with no accidents until we reached the front of her apartment.

Tink tripped and, thankfully, I had good reflexes. I caught her before she hit the ground. Holding onto one another, she had one hand on my back while the other was on my chest. We were face to face when she stared into my eyes, prompting me to return the gaze.

Out of nowhere, she leaned up and kissed me. I jumped back for a second because I wasn't one to play those kissing games with females. But something pulled me back towards her, connecting our lips again.

Our bodies came close together, and I felt my dick get hard. I ain't have no little tool, so I was sure Tink felt it pressed against her. Our kiss got more intense, as I pushed her up against the wall outside her apartment. My hands roamed around her body as hers did the same to mine.

"Come inside?" she asked between kisses.

I stopped and pulled back for a second, looking at her. "Tink, I'll fuck your whole life up," I told her.

She grabbed my chin and pecked my lips. "Fuck it up then."

"Don't say I ain't warn you."

She took the keys from my hands and opened the door. The moment we stepped foot inside, we attacked each other like two wild hyenas. Ripping clothes off one another, we got undressed in less than a minute.

I placed my gun on the center table and picked her ass up in the air. Pressing her back against the living room wall, I placed my dick at her opening while I kissed all over her neck. Her skin was so soft while her scent was intoxicating. Inching my way inside of her, she dug her nails in my back.

"Oh shit!" she yelped out.

I had one hand around her waist holding onto her while I wrapped the next around the back of her neck. Once I was all the way deep in her, I rested my face in the crook of her neck and dug in and out of her. Feeling how good she felt had me thinking about how I longed to feel inside of her since we were kids.

"Fuck," I growled.

I bit her neck as I sped up my pace. Although she was in the air, she started to fuck me back, matching my energy. Walking her to the couch with her still in my arms, I let her down, turned her around, and bent her ass over.

With one hard slap on her ass, I spread her cheeks and slid my way back inside of her. Tink threw her head back in complete bliss as her body shook. The way her ass looked with the deep arch she had in her back made me brick up more. I didn't let up not one bit. She was throwing her ass back at a nigga too, so I knew she wanted me to fuck her shit up.

I felt myself about to cum, so I grabbed a handful of her hair and sped up. Moments later, I quickly slid out of her as I shot out all my kids on her ass. She turned around and wrapped her lips around my dick to clean up the rest of it. The touch of her lips on my tool made my toes curl.

"Shit, girl. You gon' have a nigga fucked up over you," I exhaled as I caught my breath.

We both dropped on the couch as naked as we were born, gathering ourselves. No other words were spoken, but it wasn't awkward either. It wasn't even a good minute before she got on knees and crawled between my legs. With my dick still standing up, she took the whole thing in her mouth and sucked from the tip to my balls.

Round two it is.

Just as she was getting a rhythm down, I heard the door unlock. Immediately, I reached over her and grabbed my gun, aiming straight for whoever was walking in. And good thing I did; it was some nigga.

"What the fuck goin' on in here?" he raged.

TINK

When Justin walked in the door, I was completely shocked but also happy. Although having sex with Trigg was not in my plans, it felt good to get back at Justin almost immediately. The look on his face when he saw what was going on was priceless. I honestly didn't think he would've come by the apartment so soon after everything happened at the club. With the blows I gave him and Serena, I thought he would've been aiding her and his wounds, but I guess not.

"So, this the old friend you had drop you home the other day?" he asked as he stayed put by the door.

Trigg stood up and started to put on his clothes but not without moving the gun that was aimed at Justin's head. I grabbed my robe that was lying across the couch from earlier that day and put it on.

"Justin, get the fuck out," I scolded.

"What? This my fuckin' crib too. And you in here fuckin' the next nigga in it."

"Well, it ain't yours no more. I'll have yo shit packed and outta here by tomorrow."

"Bitch, you can't do that."

"Yeah, she can and she will," Trigg intervened.

"Who the fuck are you?"

Within seconds, Trigg leaped from where he stood and ran up on Justin, poking the gun under his neck. "I'm your worst nightmare, nigga. If shorty said she wants you out, then yo ass is gone. Understood?" He drove the gun deeper into his neck.

Justin didn't say a word. He just nodded.

"Good, now, get the fuck on."

As Trigg back-peddled, Justin straightened up his clothes and turned to leave out the door but not before saying his last words.

"So, you fuckin' on a street nigga and think you safe?"

"She's more than safe, and I'ma keep fuckin' on her too, my boy," Trigg answered for me.

Justin couldn't match Trigg's energy and he knew it, so he left without uttering another word. If only Justin knew what Trigg was capable of, he would've turned around the minute he opened the door and saw him.

"Thank you," I spoke softly.

"Uh huh, pack some shit and get yo ass dressed," he ordered.

"For what?" I was confused.

"Until those locks changed, I'm putting you up in one of my spots. Can't have yo momma spirit haunting me if something happened to you." He walked towards the door. "I'll be in the car, hurry up."

As soon as he left, I went and packed a bag with some clothes for a few days, threw on a sweat suit with my Uggs, and made my way downstairs in no time. When my ass landed in the passenger seat and closed the door, Trigg pulled away from the curb like a madman.

Trigg turned up the music as he drove and, while it was loud as hell, I didn't really hear it because my mind was so far gone. The mention of my mother took me back to thinking about how things would've been if she were still alive and well. Would I had been with Justin? Would Trigg and I had crossed paths again?

I looked at all the Christmas decorations people had up, making the dark place called Brooklyn light up with some holiday spirit. That time of the year I would've usually been happy and in tune, but it wasn't the case that time around. The key person to my joy was gone and, any time I saw things she loved to do for the holiday, it just broke me down even more.

We pulled up to a newly built apartment building in East New York. He led the way inside and upstairs to the apartment. When I got inside, I looked around the place and fell in love with how plush it was.

"Where your phone?" Trigg asked. I handed it to him, and he entered his number. "Hit me if you need anything, go ahead and do your thing." He started to walk back towards the apartment door.

"Wait, where you going?" I asked.

"I gotta buss a move, then home," he answered nonchalantly.

Just because we had sex, I knew it was nothing between us, even though I would've liked to think it was. "Oh, okay. I just thought you would've stayed, but be safe."

He nodded and left out the door, leaving me there all alone with my thoughts.

The following morning, I jumped out of my sleep and looked around the unfamiliar room. For a minute, I had forgotten what had gone down the night prior. I searched the bed for my phone and saw I had a million missed calls and messages from several people, mainly Maleah.

> Maleah: Treasure, please call me, I just wanna know you're good.

I shot her back a message and, within seconds, my phone rang with her name appearing on the screen requesting a facetime call. Reluctantly, I answered because I knew she wouldn't have stopped until I did.

"Bitch, what the fuck happened last night?" she started.

"And, wait, where are you?" She was looking all in my background being nosy.

My mind quickly drifted off, thinking about the sex Trigg and I had. That shit felt so good and it wasn't because it had been a minute; he knew how to break a bitch back properly.

"I'm at my..." my voice trailed off because I didn't even know what to call him, "I'm at someone's place until I get the locks on my apartment changed."

"I'm so sorry you're going through this, Tink. You don't deserve that. And I'ma still pull up to that bitch spa and drag her ass again."

"You ain't the only one. I'ma get her, I promise you."

We spoke for a few more minutes before hanging up. I got out the bed and went into the bathroom to relieve myself and wash my face. My stomach grumbled, so I headed to the kitchen to see if he had anything there.

Walking past the living room, I jumped out of fright when I saw someone sleeping on the couch but quickly relaxed when I noticed it was Trigg. He was lying there knocked out with only basketball shorts on. I didn't hear when he came back in the apartment, so I knew I was out cold.

Admiring his defined abs and all the tattoos all over his body, I was ready for another round. But before I even tried my hand, I had to test his temperature out. Trigg was the type of person to just turn cold as fuck on someone, and I didn't want to make a fool of myself.

I tiptoed my way around the kitchen and saw it had nothing in there to cook, so I turned back around and headed toward the room to get my phone. It was either going to be

UberEATS or Instacart for the win. I went and ordered us some food and took a shower.

As I was finishing up in the shower, the glass door swung open and Trigg stood there naked with his dick at attention. I tried my best not to drool but to look surprised. He stepped inside and made me face the wall. Spreading my legs apart, he swiped his hand between my legs from my pussy to my ass, then played with my clit as he bit down on my back; almost instantly, I came.

"Ughhh," I moaned out.

While still applying pressure to my button, Trigg slid his dick inside me, sending me into a complete frenzy.

"What the fuck? Oh, my God," I cried out in pleasure.

"You like that?" he asked in his deep, husky voice.

"Yes, please don't stop," I cooed.

"I won't. I told that nigga I was gon keep fuckin' on you, and I meant that."

With that being said, he bent me over more and penetrated me so deep, I felt it in my soul. He said he was going to fuck my life up, and I had a feeling he was right.

***

TWO DAYS HAD PASSED SINCE I'D SEEN TRIGG. HE LEFT ME AT HIS spot to go handle business and never returned. Our text messages and phone conversations were to a minimal. He would only answer for a hot second to make sure I was okay and went his way. I wasn't sure what I had expected; it wasn't like he was my nigga or I was his bitch.

The weekend went by and Monday arrived; I had to get the locks changed and go to the spa. I knew good and well I didn't have a job there anymore, but I had all my shit there, so I had to go and grab them. If Serena knew what was best for her, she'd just let me get my shit and leave.

Before heading to the spa, I called Maleah to see if she was free to go with me.

"Hello?" she answered.

"Hey, what you doing right now? You want to go to the spa with me to get my shit?" I asked.

"Just the action I needed, bitch. Where you at?"

"Still at this spot. Just grab me from Atlantic mall. I'm going there now," I informed her.

As soon as we hung up, I got my things situated and left out. I made sure and brought everything I owned because I wasn't sure what type of time Trigg was on. He was wishy washy and hard to read; besides, I had a place of my own and didn't need to be in his.

Taking the train to Atlantic mall, I climbed up the steps to the streets. Once I got proper phone service, I called Maleah to see where she was. As if it was perfect timing, she was pulling up to the corner where I was standing on. I hopped in her car and she drove off toward the spa, which was only a few blocks away.

"Just let me get all my shit before you do anything," I told her.

I already knew what type of timing she was on because I was on the same shit. My main concern was retrieving everything that belonged to me because I paid a lot of money for my equipment and supplies.

Maleah parked, and we got out of the car like we were getting ready to rob a bank or something. When the receptionist saw my face when I walked into the spa, it was like she saw a ghost. I bypassed her, as she tried to open her mouth and say something to me; then, I heard her dialing a number on the phone, which I assumed was Serena.

We went into my room and packed up my things as fast as possible. I heard whispers and talks amongst the other workers as they passed by my door. It was only a matter of time before Serena came and tried to start some shit. I didn't understand females like her. They loved to be wrong and strong in situations.

Maleah and I made a few trips to the car carrying my stuff. Just when we were about finished, Serena pulled up to the spa.

"Leah, just get the last box real quick," I told Maleah as I stood there in front. She ran inside and did what I asked her.

Serena approached me with a scowl on her face. "So, what's up?" she asked.

I wasn't in the mood for talking; it was only one thing I knew to do in situations like that. Something just came over me, and I took off on her. I started swinging like a madwoman, making sure each punch connected. She threw her hands back, but I was dodging them. I yanked her down to the ground by her hair and stomped her ass out.

"Yo nasty ass hoe," I spat as I kicked her ass.

Maleah and the girls from the spa ran outside and looked

on. No one dare tried to jump in. If they had, Maleah would've had a field day with their ass.

The fight went on for about two minutes until I heard police sirens blaring in our direction. I still didn't stop until I felt hands pulling me off of her. When I finally settled, I saw it was the same detectives that came and questioned me about the Uber driver's disappearance.

"Ms. King, come with us," the woman said.

"For what?" Maleah stepped in.

"She has a warrant out for assault," the male detective answered.

"This is some bullshit," I spat. "Maleah, come and get me out."

"Is this the same Maleah friend?" the woman asked. "Where were you the night of Thanksgiving?"

Maleah looked at me, and I shot her a stare.

"A friend's house for dinner, why?" Maleah answered.

"Were you with Ms. King at all that night?"

"Yes, we were together all night. I even took her home. What's this about?"

Both of the detectives looked at each other, then back at her.

"Alright, thanks for that." She seemed content.

I let out a sign of relief, but I still had another problem on my hand: being arrested.

TRIGG

"Bring me the bags. I'm outside," I told Wave.

I had just pulled up to my boy crib to collect the bags with all the merch in them. Right before, I went and grabbed two other bags from the trap, having a total of four bags for the bump man.

"I'm coming now," he told me and hung up.

A minute later, Wave was walking out of his building with both bags in his hands. He quickly shuffled his feet to get to me, trying to dodge the cold weather. I popped the trunk, rested the bags inside, and closed it.

"It's fuckin' brick city out this bitch," he joked as he hopped in the passenger side.

"No cap, shit crazy out here," I agreed, dapping him up.

I pulled off in the direction to meet the bump man. The nigga been blowing up my phone for a few days to get the merch, but I still had my guys swiping and getting more shit.

"Yo, I meant to ask, you still want niggas on shorty?" Wave questioned.

I thought about it for a moment. After fuckin' Tink, I had a feeling she wasn't going to be on no bullshit when it came to running her mouth. She was never the type, and it looked like she was the same way.

"Nah, you can tell 'em stay off her," I ordered. At that point, if the law had pulled up on her again about the situation, she would've told me.

Wave got on his phone and made the phone call but, instead of speaking, he was doing most of the listening. "Aight, I'll hit your line in a second," he spoke and hung up. "Aye, shorty was just arrested," he revealed.

"Arrested? For what?" I jumped up in my seat.

"She was out there tussling with some bitch at her job."

God damn, Tink, I shook my head.

"Tell him stay on her still," I decided. "Let's go and get rid of this shit, so I can go see what the fuck going on with her."

"You checking for shorty now or something?" Wave eyed me.

"Fuckin' her, yeah. And that pussy A1, so I gotta make sure it's available when I want it."

"Damnnn, son. I see you. No wonder you ain't worried 'bout her running her mouth no more. She bad as fuck, too."

"Real shit."

We both laughed and dapped each other up. I didn't

mention that I knew Tink from back in the days; everything didn't need to be spoken on. And, although we had history, I wasn't trying to get too attached to her or have her get attached to me. My lifestyle and ways were bad for her so, if we could've just kept it simple, fuck and kick it for a few, everything would be just fine. A nigga ain't have time for all that lovey dovey shit.

Wave and I chopped it up the whole ride to the city. When we reached the parking garage where we always met the bump man, he was already parked up and waiting. I pulled into the spot right next to him and hopped out.

"Trigg, wassup?" Levi greeted me.

"Shit, you know the vibes."

Wave and Levi greeted each other, and we got right down to business. Opening the trunk, I unzipped the bags and exposed the contents inside. Levi's eyes lit up like it was already Christmas. He briefly searched through the bags and, in the end, as always, agreed to take everything.

We did the exchange, then went and got in the whip. As I was pulling out, I saw Tink's boyfriend or ex, whatever the fuck he was to her, driving past me. When I looked in the rearview mirror, I saw he was meeting up with Levi.

Small fuckin' world, I thought. Seeing him let me know what kind of business he was into and where I could catch his ass if he ever thought he wanted smoke. Shaking him from the forefront of my mind, I pressed on the gas to get back to Brooklyn to see what the hell was going on with Tink.

Once I dropped Wave off, I called Tink's phone to see if she answered but, instead, her homegirl from the club answered.

"Where Tink at?" I asked.

"She got arrested," she stated. "I'm at the precinct now waiting for them to release her."

"What precinct is it?"

"Eighty-forth."

"Aight, bet." I hung up and made my way over there.

I wasn't sure what the fuck was up with Tink, but it seemed like she had shit rough for her. Every time she turned around, it was something else. Whatever it was, I needed her to tighten up and get her shit together. She was on my mind the entire ride downtown. I had this weird feeling of needing to protect her from wherever and whoever, but I knew better than to get too close.

When I reached the precinct, I stayed put in the car. Walking up in that building wasn't in my plans. Shit was too risky. Besides, places like that made my muthafuckin' skin crawl.

Ringing Tink's phone again, her girl answered. "She's coming out right now," she spoke as soon as the call connected.

"Bet, I'm outside." I stepped out of the car and waited for them to exit the building.

A few minutes later, both ladies came walking out hand in hand. Tink looked like she was just out of it and defeated.

"Shorty!" I called out to her.

When she looked up and saw me, her face looked like it melted away all the worries she had.

"What you doing here?" she asked in a surprised toned.

"I got the news, so I had to pull up."

"Oh, thanks."

"Where you finna go?" I looked at her and her friend.

"Ummm, me and Maleah gotta go get locks for the door, then going home," she informed me.

"You got someone to put it on?"

She shook her head no.

"Aight, go get it and I'll meet y'all back at ya crib to change it," I offered.

"Okay." She gave me a shy smile and walked away.

I hopped back in my vee and went to make a move before heading to her place.

WHEN I SPUN THE BLOCK AND REACHED BACK AT TINK'S, I SAW the building door was open so I let myself in and went upstairs. From outside her door, I could hear her talking to her friend, Maleah. The two were speaking about her current predicament, having no job, the breakup with that dickhead ass nigga and, of course, me.

"Man, if Justin would've given me the money he promised me for the own spa and recovery house, I would've been good. Now, I'm fucked and don't know which way to turn," Tink voiced.

"Aht, aht, we're not doing that, boo. You will find a way, you always do," Maleah convinced her.

"I guess."

"Mmmhmm, and wassup with you and ol' boy?"

"Nothing, for real."

"Yeah, aight. I'm not stupid."

I stood there long enough to hear a good amount of shit but not too long where I would've been considered a weirdo.

Knock! Knock!

A few seconds later, Maleah opened the door, stepped aside, and let me in.

"Aight, I gotta make a move. I'll talk to you later," Maleah told Tink as she left out the apartment.

"Where's the lock?" I asked, holding the door open so I could switch it out.

Tink went over and grabbed a bag from off her dining table and brought it over to me. I got right down to business and started to change the locks. She sat there quiet, looking on while I worked.

"So, what's good? You gon' tell me what's going on or what?" I came out and asked.

She was getting into a lot of shit and, while I knew it may have stemmed from her ex, I wanted to hear it from her mouth.

"I doubt you want to hear it," she tried to brush off the subject.

"I wouldn't have asked." I continued to work on the locks.

She shifted in her seat, took a deep breath in, and let it out. "Long story short, I caught Justin, my now ex, cheating with my boss. The night at the club was when I saw them and ran in their heads. Then, when I went to go get my shit from work, she pulled up on some rah rah shit, so I ran in her mouth," she explained.

"Oh, so you a whole gangsta then, huh?" I joked, making her laugh.

"I mean, I be chilling, but they deserved that shit."

"I feel you. You gotta know when to act out of character and when not to."

"Yeah, like you, right? Gotta do what you gotta do?" She eyed me.

Without saying anything, I knew she was referring to how I did ol' boy the night of Thanksgiving. I never felt bad for doing anything I was supposed to when someone tried to play with me.

"Right. And I'll always stand on business, shorty," I spoke sternly.

I finished changing the locks and double checked it to make sure it was working properly. "You all set now," I told her as I handed over the new keys.

"Thanks Trigg, your lady real lucky," she stated.

"Nah, ain't no such thing. I don't believe in that."

"What the hell you mean?" She cocked her head to the side.

"Just what I said. The life I live, I can't have no woman. It's just how it is." I shrugged.

"But you can fuck 'em?" She raised a brow.

"Yeah, just like I'm finna fuck you."

I was over all the talking nonsense. Closing the distance

between us, I hovered over her short frame. She looked up at me with the most innocent eyes ever, but I knew better than to be a fool.

"Baby girl, you gon' suck it or not?" I spoke, quoting Cam'ron.

Without hesitation, she dropped to her knees and did what she had to do.

TINK

"Don't run, Tink, take this dick," Trigg growled.

"Fuckkk!" I screamed.

We were on round five at that point, with neither of us trying to tap out. He grabbed a handful of my hair, yanking my head back as he pressed his other hand on my back to make it arch even more. I felt all of him inside me, almost as if his dick was about to reach my throat.

It had been days of non-stop fucking; Trigg had me gone, gone real bad. Anyone other than him had never touched and penetrated me in that way. He exposed me to new sexual heights, making me never wanting to lie down with anyone else ever again.

He slid out of me and flipped me over so I was lying on

my back. Lifting both my legs up above my head, he slid back in me, working his hips in a circular motion. Feeling myself about to cum for the thousandth time, he wrapped his hand around my neck, leaned down, and stuck his tongue in my mouth, all while still working his dick in and out of me. I immediately exploded and creamed all over him.

The shit Trigg did made me want to just give my life to him, marry him, and live happily ever after. But he wasn't into all of that. He was content with just the sex, and I was too, for the moment.

"Fuck, I'm 'boutta come." He laid his face in the crook of my neck. "Damn, this shit feels good."

His voice, his touch, and his scent always sent me into a frenzy, especially when it was in the bed. Trigg picked up his pace and, moments later, I felt his dick pulsate as he came inside of me. It was the first time he had ever done so without a condom. For a minute, he just stayed put while still in me, catching his breath. Finally, he pulled out and laid on his back.

Both of us looked up at the ceiling in our own thoughts. I knew in his mind he probably was thinking he slipped up coming in me because what if I had gotten pregnant? He didn't want a relationship or a consistent woman in his life, so a baby was far from the equation.

Out of nowhere, he jumped up and went into the bathroom. I heard the shower running, so I knew he was about to get cleaned up. The only difference was, we'd usually shower together and get another round in while we were at it.

Instead of going to join him, I stayed put in the bed until he was done, so I could get myself together.

About ten minutes later, Trigg came back into the room and started putting on his clothes. He didn't look my way, nor did he say anything to me. It was a weird tension in the air, and I had a mind it was about him not being strong enough to pull out; that's what good coochie did.

"You leaving?" I came out and questioned.

He didn't answer me; instead, he continued to get ready in silence. Once he got completely dressed and heading to the door to put his sneakers on, I jumped off the bed, wrapped my robe around my body and approached him.

"What's your whole thing? You were just good," I pressed, yet he gave no response. I reached out to grab his arm and, in one swift motion, he pinned me up against the wall.

"Keep yo fuckin' hands to yourself," he grilled.

"Did I do something wrong?" I felt tears welling up in my eyes.

He looked at me for a moment, and his grip on my arms softened until he let me go completely.

"Nah, but I'm out." He opened the door and stormed out.

All sorts of things were running through my mind. I just left a hurtful relationship and was then involved with someone who didn't want shit but my pussy. I couldn't have been mad, though. I knew what it was from the jump; I chose to deal with it.

"Maaaa!" I yelled out, wishing she was there to help guide me.

My phone rang, quickly pulling me out of my emotions for the moment. I raced to the room to answer it before it stopped ringing. "Hello?" I picked up the unknown call.

"Hi, Treasure King?" the woman asked.

"Yes, who's speaking?"

"This is Ms. Brown from St. Mary's home. I was calling to see if you were going to attend the annual Christmas celebration your mother always done. It's now celebrated in her honor."

Time and time again, the reality of my mother being gone just kept slapping me in the face. While I was happy to hear they were going to continue the Christmas celebration in her honor, it also saddened me she couldn't attend.

"Oh, I did not know. Sure, I will be there," I confirmed.

I had nothing planned for the holidays anyway. There was no man in my life or no kids. I didn't even have a job.

"Great, it's on Christmas Eve. Please feel free to bring anything for the kids. We'd appreciate all things."

"No problem. See you then."

I finally had something to look forward to. Almost immediately, my mind started thinking about what to donate and what to wear.

Mommy, I'll make you proud, I thought.

***

"Oooh, grab that one, it's so cute," I told Maleah.

My girl and I were out shopping for the kids at the home. I decided to dig into my savings that I had put aside for my own spa to get the entire home something. Right after I hung up with Ms. Brown, I dialed her back and had her send me all the ages and sex of the kids.

"Yes, it is. Man, these kids gon be so happy. This is dope, sis." Maleah smiled. "But, wait, run that shit back to me. He bussed in you then bussed out the crib?"

"Girl, yeah." I shook my head.

Trigg been on my mind lately, and I was just trying to figure out what the fuck was his problem. The way he acted and move, I knew it was something deep-rooted in him, I just didn't know what.

"Treasure, what's gon' happen if yo ass gets pregnant? He don't even want a girl. What the fuck he gon' do with a kid?"

"Leah, I don't know. Shit, it's partially my fault. I should've tried to get him off me, but that shit was feeling so good." I started to think about our times tangled in the sheets.

"See, and that's why yo hot ass in this predicament you in now." She shot me a look.

Just when I was about to respond, my phone chimed a couple of times, indicating I had text messages.

> Jus: Treasure, baby. Can we talk?
>
> Jus: I fucked up, I know, but I miss the shit outta you.
>
> Jus: Just please let a nigga holla at you for a minute.
>
> Jus: Please.

Turning the phone in Maleah's direction, I showed her the messages from Justin.

"He ain't serious, is he?" She screwed her face up.

"I have no clue, but I ain't with none of that. I'm good."

"Better not be."

"Let's finish this shopping; we have mad shit to get still," I told her.

As we shopped for the kids, we continued to talk about everything that had been going on with me and some with her. I opened up and told her where I knew Trigg from, but I kept out the part about Thanksgiving night. That's something I would go to the grave with.

After we cashed out, we loaded up Maleah's car, which we thought everything wasn't going to fit but we made it happen. She headed over to my place to drop me off. Since she lived in a house with only a few steps to go up, we agreed that it would be smart if she took the gifts home and had her brothers help her get them inside. The following day, I would go over and help wrap and bag them up.

"Thanks so much, Leah," I told her, as she pulled up to my building.

"Girl, please. I'll see you tomorrow."

We gave each other a hug, and I left out her car and made my way upstairs. When I reached my floor, I saw Justin standing in front of my door.

What the fuck?

"What are you doing here?" I quizzed with irritation.

"You wouldn't answer my calls or texts, fuck else am I supposed to do?"

"Ummm, leave me alone."

"I can't do that, ma. I need you. I'm sorry, man," he pleaded.

"Too late, now, excuse me." I slightly pushed him out my way, so I could get inside.

"Treasure, I'll do anything to make it up to you. Please." He grabbed my arm to make me face him. That's when I saw tears rolling down his face, but it didn't faze me not one bit.

"Get the fuck off of me." I snatched my arm away.

Opening the door, I rushed inside and closed it quickly as possible. He stood on the other side banging and pleading until he finally gave up.

"You know what? Fuck you, bitch. Don't come running back when that nigga fucks you over," he spat and walked off, as I heard his footsteps descend.

I let out a sigh of relief but, immediately after, I busted into tears. All I wanted to do was to be happy, healthy, successful, and drama free.

TRIGG

"Them niggas finished breaking down the product?" I asked Wave, who was driving at the moment.

"Yeah. I told them we were finna pull up now," he confirmed.

"Aight, let's go in here and see what's what."

When a lot of things were on my mind, I had a habit of drowning myself in work and staying busy. And at that point, I needed to keep Tink off my mind. Wave and I had been busy bussing moves non-stop. We even ended up going out of town for a quick two-day trip to handle some things. All this time, I didn't speak to Tink at all since I left her spot.

Entering the trap spot, I looked around and saw niggas lounging and goofing around. At first, I decided not to say anything but, when I walked in further and noticed they weren't finished bagging up the product, I felt some kind of way, and I hated when I felt like someone was playing with me.

"What the fuck going on in here?" I barked.

Everyone stopped what they were doing and had their eyes fixed on me.

"I ain't talkin' to myself, son. Why the hell this shit not ready?" I went on.

"We're almost finished, Tee, hold on," one of the young niggas stated.

"What the fuck you just said?" I turned to face him, but he never answered. I pulled my gun out of my waistband and pointed it at him. "I said, what the fuck you just said, my nigga?"

"It's almost finished," he quickly spoke with his hands in the air.

"Nah, son, you told me to hold on. Don't ever in your fuckin' life tell me to do shit." I shoved the gun in the center of his forehead.

Wave stepped in front of me and shot me a look that said to chill. After contemplating on if I wanted to make an example out of the lil' nigga or not, I decided to back down. When I couldn't think straight, I usually acted on impulse.

"Go ahead in the vee, bro, I got it," Wave told me.

I nodded, turned around, and headed for the door. All eyes were still stuck on me with every step that I took. Those niggas knew not to play with me, and I had to do everything to keep that fear and respect in them.

Returning to my vee, I hopped in the passenger seat since Wave was driving all day. I needed to light a blunt and get a drink of some Dusse or something to take the edge off. After the last move for the day, I was going to get low and chill.

A text message that came in pulled me from my thoughts; it was from Tink. I told myself it was a long paragraph or book of some kind girls loved to text; I wasn't even going to open it. But when I peeped it was a simple, quick text and what it entailed, it alarmed me.

> Tink: Justin just came by my crib on some crazy shit. I don't know what to do.

Immediately, I called Wave's phone and told him to let's go. We would spin the block later and go handle the product. I needed to get to Tink as soon as possible.

> Me: I'm on my way.

WHEN I GOT ABOUT TWO BLOCKS AWAY, I CALLED TINK'S PHONE.

"Hello?" she answered.

I heard the uneasiness in her voice. "I'm finna pull up," I told her.

"Okay."

By the time I arrived in front of her building, she was already downstairs in some shorts and a jacket.

"What the hell you doing outside?" I questioned her as I made my way to her stoop. She came walking down and stood right in front of me, one step up.

"I don't know. Staying in that place was sending me crazy. I never saw Justin like that before," she started to ramble.

"Aye, aye, relax. What happened?"

"When I came home from being out with Maleah, he was just standing there in front of my door. He was begging for me to take him back and all kinds of wild shit, even was crying. Then, he tried to grab me, but I got out his grip and got inside."

Hearing the wild shit ol' boy did pissed me off. I hated when niggas didn't know when to just move the fuck around and keep it stepping. And that stalker shit wasn't cool, it was weird and dangerous.

"Aight, calm down. I'ma handle it."

In the act of trying to ease her mind, I saw her eyes grow wide like gulf balls. Instantly, she pushed me to the ground, and that's when I heard gunshots ringing out. Her body dropped onto mine, and I immediately assumed the worst. I held onto her tight until the shots stopped and tires screech off into the distances.

"Trigg!" I heard Wave yell out to me.

I didn't even pay him any mind. My focus was Tink. "Tink, you good?" I asked, raising her up.

"Trigg, you got hit," she spoke lowly.

I looked down and saw there was blood on my white shirt, so her eyes started to tear up. Quickly patting myself down, I realize it wasn't my blood, so it had to be hers, which had me worried.

"It's not mine. Come here." I started to search her body, and that's when I noticed she was grazed on her arm.

"Oh my God, I got shot," she started to panic and cry.

"Chill out, Tink, damn. You just got grazed," I told her.

"What you wanna do? We gotta get outta here before twelve come," Wave suggested, still surveying the area.

"You locked your door?" I asked Tink.

She nodded, wiping her tears away with the uninjured hand.

"Call Doctor Green and tell him to meet us at my spot," I instructed Wave.

He got on the line and dialed him up right away.

"We're not going to the hospital?" she asked, as I led her to the car.

"Nah, that's too hot. Don't worry, I got you," I assured her.

On God, after what had just gone down, I was going to forever make sure Tink was good.

After I got in her the backseat, I hopped in the passenger while Wave took the wheel and pulled off.

***

"What we gon' do about this nigga?" Wave asked as he passed me the blunt.

I took a couple of puffs and let it out into the air as I tried to relax a bit. The way my mind was racing, I was ready to kill anything walking. After a few minutes into the ride to my place, I let her calm down a bit before I asked her who she saw. It wasn't a rocket science question, but I just needed to hear it from her mouth. She said it was Justin.

"Hit Levi and get the drop on son. I don't care about his price," I answered.

"Say less."

Seconds later, Doctor Green came walking out of the bedroom to where Wave and I sat.

"Trigg, she's fine. Just make sure to keep changing the dressing. I gave her some antibiotics and mild pain meds. Make sure she takes them," he instructed. "If anything seems wrong, just call me."

"Thanks a lot, Doc." I stood to my feet and shook his hand.

Doctor Green been on my payroll for a while. He was great at his job and loyal. I never had to worry about him running his mouth to anyone when I called him to handle crazy situations. He asked no questions, only ones pertaining to getting the patient better.

As Doctor Green was heading out the door, Wave jumped up to feet. "I'ma slide bro. Go be with shorty. I'll get things lined up and let you know what's good."

"Aight bet." We dapped each other up and he left out.

I plopped back down on the couch and finished the blunt Wave and I was smoking earlier, allowing Tink to invade my mind. From the moment she saved a nigga life and almost sacrificed herself for me, something was triggered within me.

I started to feel something, something I hadn't felt since a little boy.

While I kept trying to tell myself not to take it there with her, my heart kept telling me something different. It was the first time my heart ever spoke to me when it came to a woman. I never had feelings; I didn't want to. And no female ever sparked the want or need for me to feel until Tink.

"Trigg?" I heard her soft voice call out to me from the bedroom.

"Yo, I'm coming," I told her.

Finishing up the blunt, I outed it and rest it in the ashtray. I got up from the couch and went into my bedroom where Tink was. She was laid up under the comforter watching TV. I walked over to her side and sat on the edge of the bed.

"Wassup, you good?" I asked her, slightly touching her wounded arm.

"Yeah, I'm good. It doesn't even hurt for real."

"Mmm, okay gangsta."

We both started to laugh. I was happy as hell she was in a good mood and not all fucked up in the head about what happened. Deep down inside, I knew she was hurting and was just trying to play things cool on the surface.

"Thanks for getting the doctor here for me."

"Fuck all lat, Treasure. Thank you for saving a nigga life tonight." I scooted up closer to her. "What the fuck was running through your mind to even act like that?"

She got quiet and hung her head, but I quickly raised it back up with my index finger. "Wassup, talk to me," I pushed. I really wanted to know.

"Treyce, sorry, Trigg—"

"You said it right the first time," I cut her off, causing her to smile at my statement.

"Treyce, I just couldn't stomach losing someone else. I don't have much of friends and no family. Even though the way we reconnected was wild as fuck, I'm happy we did. And, honestly, I've loved you since I was a young girl, so you weren't finna catch a bullet, especially not because of my stupidity," she expressed.

Hearing those words come out of her mouth only confirmed my assumptions about her feelings towards me and solidified my feelings for her.

"First, you ain't do nothing stupid but love a nigga that didn't know how to love you. It ain't your fault your pussy hold power and got muthafuckers ready to end lives. Shit, I just fell in line. I'll end the world behind that shit," I joked but was serious.

She bussed out laughing hysterically.

"Nah, on some G shit, I fuck with you, Treasure. I ain't never felt like this about nobody. After I witnessed my moms getting murdered because niggas couldn't find her dude, I always told myself I wasn't gon' put a woman in that predicament. I—"

"What? I'm so sorry Treyce, no wonder you act the way you do," she blurted out.

If it was anyone else, I probably would've snapped. But Tink understood me, and I knew the statement came from the heart. "I guess." I nodded my head slowly.

"And that's alright, it's always room for change and

growth, but that's only if you want it," she schooled. "Let me in, Treyce. Let me help you heal. Let me love you." She took my hand in hers.

Little did she know, I already had my mind set on letting her in. The first step was me revealing details about my mother's murder. I never spoke on that to no one.

"Treasure, don't fuck with a nigga heart. I'll kill you for real, and I won't miss. And I promise to do any and everything necessary to keep you safe and happy," I expressed.

"I promise I won't."

"Aight. Now, come bring me them lips."

"Which ones?" She looked between her legs, then back at me with a smirk.

"Lil' nasty ass. I'll take both."

Leaning in, I kissed her lips softly as she grabbed ahold of my face, bringing my body onto hers. Undressing each other as our tongues tussled, we were naked in our birthday suits in no time. I wanted her more than I ever did before; it was a weird ass feeling, but I accepted it.

I landed kisses on her neck while my hands roamed around her body and made its way between her legs. Before I touched her pussy, I knew she was wet. I felt the heat seeping from between her thighs when I was lying on her. Playing with her clit, I slipped a finger inside her and twirled it around, making her move underneath me all the while still attacking her neck.

Accidentally hitting her injured arm, I jumped back.

"My fault."

"Boy, fuck this arm. Do you," she stated, causing us both to chuckle.

With that being said, I made my way down her chest, stopping to kiss on her full breasts. Then, I made my way down to her stomach and finally the prize. I blew on her clit right before I passed my tongue from her opening to her clit.

"Oooh, shiittt," she moaned out.

I went in for the kill and latched onto her nob and sucked it until I felt her moving her hips in a circular motion. While Tink thrust her hips up towards my face, I applied pressure onto her clit and finger fucked her, sending her into complete bliss. Her warm fluid came leaking out, letting me know I did what I had to do.

"Baby, I want you inside me," she cooed.

Hearing her call me that only made me want to fuck her more. It didn't make me cringe like it usually would have with someone else.

I turned her to lie on her good side as I got behind her. Lifting her leg up in the air, I positioned my dick at her opening and slowly inched my way in. With her lying on my other hand, I cupped her face back to me and kissed her ass in the nastiest way ever while I gave her long, deep strokes.

"Mmmm," she moaned.

"You like that?" I whispered in her ear.

She looked back at me in my eyes and said, "Yes, daddy."

I got her on all fours without taking my dick out of her and fucked her so good. My goal was when I was finished with her, any other nigga before me was going to be a far distant memory. Tink was officially mine.

AFTER WHAT FELT LIKE FOREVER, TINK AND I WERE KNOCKED OUT cold. Once I saw she was comfortable and resting well, I felt content enough in the moment to get some shut eye myself. I thought I would've been asleep until the morning, but I realized that wasn't the case when Wave called my phone at one o'clock in the morning.

"This better be good," I answered, irritated.

"It is. Got the drop on that nigga," he revealed.

I jumped up, forgetting that Tink was lying on my chest. "Shit, my fault, baby," I told her and got her back comfortable on a pillow.

Sliding out of the bed, I went out into the living to holler at Wave. "Right now?" I quizzed.

"Mmmhmm, what you wanna do?"

"Get the renty and pull up on me," I instructed him, referring to a rental car we had on standby for certain runs. When we were finished using them, we'd get them scrapped, then go and get a new one. They were never taken out on real names, so nothing ever traced back to us.

"Bet."

In the meantime, I started to roll up a blunt. When I was done and ready to spark it, I decided to check on Tink first. I went to the bedroom door, which was ajar, looked inside and saw her still sleeping peacefully. She was the most gorgeous ass female I'd ever come across. And I felt that way from the first time I laid eyes on her at the foster home.

Making a big step and allowing change in my life when it

came to love and women was scary. But there was no doubt in my mind that I chose the right person to expose me to everything I was once against. Treasure was not only beautiful inside and out, but she was also smart, had goals, ambitious, had her head on right, loyal, a rider and, most of all, a real ass bitch.

I went inside the bedroom and into the closet to grab a quick fit. Quietly, I went over to her and kissed her on her forehead. She stirred in her sleep a little but didn't wake up. I left out the room and made sure to close the door behind me.

Returning to the living room, I got dressed in the sweats I pulled out and threw on some Jordans to match. I sparked up the blunt I rolled and puffed on it until Wave pulled up.

"You spoke to Tanz?" I asked Wave, referring to my boy who owned Starlets.

"Yeah, he's hipped."

The information Wave got from our bump man, Levi, was that Justin found himself at Starlets. I wasn't sure if the nigga was just stupid to be out in the open after pulling some shit like he did, or did he think that was going to be an alibi for him if Tink got the law involved? It was explained to us that he went to the club early, being one of the first set of people inside.

"Pass me that silencer," I told Wave, tucking it in my back pocket. "Aight, we out."

We both jumped out of the rental, which we parked up a

few blocks down from the club, and walked up. When we reached the premises, we went to the back and was let through the backdoor that had a hidden camera that only Tanz knew about. It was perfect for us to get in and out undetected.

"He's in the section on the right of the DJ booth," the guard who was instructed to let us in informed us.

"Get one girl to take him in the cut for me." I handed over a wad of money to him.

Wave and I moved quickly through the club and got in the spot where the dancer would lead him too. Patiently waiting, it wasn't long before he came our way trailing behind the pussy he thought he was finna get.

The moment he reached the point where he was out of sight of the club's floor, Wave snatched him and brought him down to the ground. The dancer nodded her head and ran along, leaving us to handle our business.

Once he was on the floor and Wave and I were hovering over him, I gave him a few seconds to see who the fuck it was before I started to beat the shit out of him. We stomped his ass thin into the fuckin' floor. With every kick, punch, and stomp, I felt some anger release, but I wasn't finished yet.

I grabbed the silencer from my back pocket and screwed it on my gun. While lying there bloody but still alert, I squatted down to his level and pushed the silencer in his mouth.

"If you ever think about speaking to Tink again, just make your funeral arrangements. And if you dare shoot at me or her again, you might as well turn the fuckin' gun on yourself. Understood?" I threatened, loud enough for him to hear me.

He nodded his head up and down, fast as shit.

"Oh, one more thing. Tell your lil' Spanish girlfriend she better have those charges dropped. I don't think I have to tell you what will happen if not."

"Uh huh," I heard him say in a muffled tone.

I wanted to blow his fuckin' brains out so badly, but I told Tink I wanted to change. And thinking about her made me go another route when handling him.

Standing back up, I looked down at his already fucked up appearance and started to walk off. But the devil on my left shoulder didn't allow me to. Plus, my trigger finger was itching like hell. I spun around, aimed at his hand, and sent a single bullet in it.

"Uggghhhhh. What the fuck?" he screamed out above the music.

"That's for not keeping your hands to yourself, nigga."

"They don't call yo ass Trigg for nothing, nigga," Wave joked loudly.

"On God, you already know. We out though."

CHAPTER 9

TINK

My mother always told me there's always a storm before things brighten up. At one point, I didn't know if I was coming or going mentally. My faith slipped just a little but was quickly restored. I lost my man and my job all at once but gained someone and something so much bigger and better.

The shooting was a blessing in disguise. Instead of making things worse, it only made Trigg and me closer. It was as if Justin's intention was for the shot to hurt one of us, but it didn't; it shattered the cold wall Trigg had up.

When he opened up about his mother, that's when I knew I had him. His story was always hidden while he spent time at the home. Most people were known for where they came from or what situation they came from, but Trigg's past was shut tight like a vault.

After our heart to heart, we had the most amazing sex. The way my body reacted to him was different from anyone else. It was like I was made to be with him. No matter how sore I felt, I wanted him inside of me, touching me, kissing me. So, when I woke up in the middle of the early morning and didn't see him in bed or in the condo overall, I frowned because I thought he had pulled one on me again and ran.

I reached for my phone on the nightstand and called his phone, but I heard it ringing in the living room. When I went out there, I saw it tucked in between the couch.

What the fuck? Where the fuck are you? I thought.

Just when I started to become dismayed and confused, the door to the condo unlocked and Trigg walked in.

"What's wrong?" He rushed over to me.

"Nothing, nothing, I'm fine," I tried to brush it off and not look crazy.

"Treasure, what happened?"

I looked into his eyes and saw he was truly concerned. "I thought you ran off on me again. When—"

He pulled me into his embrace and hugged me tight, cutting my sentence short. "I ain't going nowhere, baby girl. Don't trip, aight?"

I looked up at him and nodded. He leaned down and gave me a nice, slow kiss. As I was hugging him, I felt his gun on his waist, which prompted me to inquire about his whereabouts.

"Wait, where were you?" I asked.

"I had to handle some business," he simply answered and smiled.

I left it at that and didn't question him further. When we returned to the bedroom, he stripped out of his clothes and went to take a shower. After seeing his dick get hard from a distance, I couldn't help but to join him. That turned into multiple rounds of mind-blowing sex into the bright early morning.

THE FOLLOWING AFTERNOON, SINCE WE SLEPT IN LATE AND ignored the world, Trigg and I finally woke up. Tangled in each other's arms, we landed kissed all over one another.

"Good morning, beautiful," he whispered in my ear.

"Good morning, handsome."

He got out of bed and went for his phones that were on the dresser. Holding both of them in his hands and scrolling, his face turned into a surprised expression.

"Everything cool?" I pried.

"Yeah, I just didn't notice it's Christmas Eve tomorrow," he expressed.

"Oh shit, it is." I jumped out of the bed. "I gotta get to Maleah's house to help her wrap the gifts for St. Mary's Home."

I didn't even wait to hear his response to what I had said. Rushing into the bathroom, brushing my teeth, washing my face, and hopping in the shower was my priority at that time. Once I was finished showering, I realized I had no clothes to change into. After the shooting, I went straight to Trigg's place. When I bathed, he gave me boxers and a t-shirt to put on.

"I don't have any clothes," I whined, coming out the bathroom.

Trigg was on the phone with someone but told them to hold. "I'll give you a sweatsuit to put on and some socks," he quickly offered before returning to his call.

With nothing but the towel wrapped around my body, I went ahead and applied lotion to my skin and pulled my hair into a messy bun. By that time, Trigg got off the phone and went into his closet to grab me a sweatsuit.

"What color are your feets?" he asked, referring to my footwear.

"Tan," I answered.

"Got chu."

Moments later, he walked out holding a tan on black Nike Tech. Watching it closely, I knew I would fit into it perfectly. Trigg had a tall and athletic build. His clothes gave me just enough loose room to have a comfortable but not oversized look.

I thanked him for the clothes and quickly got dressed. Calling Maleah was next on my to-do list. She had no idea of what happened the night before, no one did. But she was going to receive all the tea I had to pour once I got with her.

"Hey, boo. I started wrapping the gifts already. When you coming?" Maleah answered as soon as the call connected.

"I'm coming now. I just finished getting dressed."

Trigg was still busy on the phone handling his business,

so I didn't want to bother him with having to drop me off. "Baby, I'll see you later. I'm leaving to go to Leah's," I told him.

"Aye, nigga, hold on," he told the person on the phone. "How you getting there? She came to pick you up?"

"No, I'm taking the train and bus."

"Hell no. Hold on." He got up from his seat in the living room and took off to the bedroom. Not long after, he was walking towards me with a Nike Tech on, similar to the one I had with just a different color.

"Baby, you don't have—"

"I do. Now, bring that ass on." He slapped me hard on my butt as we headed for the door.

We made our way downstairs and to his car. I gave him Maleah's address, sat back, and enjoyed the ride. Trigg played his trap music the first half of the ride until I asked him to listen to some kind of Christmas music, like Mariah Carey for example. He shot me a look but gave in and let me bump my choice of songs. I was finally in a holiday spirit, so I needed the vibe to match.

When he dropped me off at Maleah's, he told me to have her come outside for him to holler at her for a quick second. At first, I was confused because the two didn't know each other, only through me. But he was adamant on speaking with her and told me to mind my business.

I went inside and told Maleah he wanted to speak and, of course, she was also surprised but went outside because I told her to. The two of them spoke for a few minutes before she came back into the house.

"What was that about?" I questioned skeptically.

"He gave me some babysitting rules. You got some stuff you want to tell me?" She eyed me.

I wasn't sure what Trigg told her and to what extent, but I knew I had to cough up everything that happened. We got comfortable in the living room and started wrapping, and I started talking.

CHRISTMAS EVE

"Is that all the gifts?" I asked Maleah.

We had just finished loading up her car once again with all the children's things. That time around, the final destination was the home and in their hands.

"Yes, that's all," she answered. "Let's go."

We hopped in the car and headed to the home, which wasn't too far from where Maleah nor I stayed. Getting there wasn't a hassle and, thankfully, we made it on time.

"Treasure, you made it," Ms. Brown greeted me in the front of the home.

"Of course, I wouldn't miss it."

"I'm glad. The kids are having a ball inside. We had an unexpected surprise of donations for the celebration, so I was able to give them a full party."

"Oh yeah? That's dope, so happy that happened."

Maleah and I carried as many bags of gifts as we could the first round, but we knew we were going to have to go back for the rest. Walking into the home, music was bumping, and the kids were running around playing with one another while the teens were ducked off in the corner vibing. It reminded me of the old times when my mom was the manager, and I visited.

Being back at St. Mary's without her felt odd, but I felt her spirit beside me. I knew she was looking down at me, smiling and yelling to her fellow angels, "That's my daughtaaa or whatever." I smiled at the thought.

"Treasure, come and meet the gentleman who came and blessed us along with you for the holidays," Ms. Brown suggested.

I looked at Maleah, and she just shrugged. Following Ms. Brown into the kitchen to meet the other donor, Leah trailed right behind. And when I saw who it was, my heart instantly burst into joy.

"Treyce, what are you doing here?" I asked with excitement, rushing over to him for a hug and kiss.

"I listened to you yesterday when you were in a frantic state about wrapping the gifts for the kids here. So, I hollered at Maleah to find out more about what you were doing. I then called up the home, spoke with Ms. Brown, and asked how I could've been of help as well," he explained.

"Y'all sneaky as hell." I pointed at Trigg and Leah, causing everyone to laugh. "But, nah, I really love this. Thanks so much for coming through for these kids, baby."

"I was once here, literally. And I know for a fact Ms. King would've wanted me to give back."

He made me fall for him all over again. I had no words. I just looked at him with pure admiration.

"But, shorty, I got a surprise for you," he came out and revealed.

"Huh? What is it?"

He took my hand and led me out of the house with Maleah, Ms. Brown, his friend Wave, and a few of the older kids following behind. We walked a few buildings over and stopped in front of a two-story commercial building.

"What's going on?" I was confused.

Trigg proceeded to hand me a gift-wrapped box. I opened it and saw it had a key inside. He handed me an envelope and told me to open it, so I did. It read:

Merry Christmas, Beautiful,

You deserve the world and more, and I'm willing to be the person who gives it to you. Keep chasing your dreams and let no one or anything get in the way of you doing so. I will make sure of it, too. Thanks for never giving up on me and always having my back, literally. I love you.

P.S. That's your building for your spa and recovery home and a check to fund it. Live your dreams baby girl.

"WHAT?" I SQUEALED OUT LOUD BEFORE HOPPING INTO HIS arms. "Babyyy, thank you, thank you, thank you."

"Ain't shit, baby girl. Just make me and your moms proud," he told me.

"I will, I will. You really just melted my whole heart with this one."

"Nah, you melted the heart of a menace and remade that shit. And for that, I thank you."

"I love you, Treyce." I pecked his lips.

"I love you more, Treasure."

"So, y'all gon leave us in the cold or you gon' open the door, Treasure?" Maleah blurted out.

"Oh, my fault y'all."

I inserted the key and turned the lock to my very own place of business, thanks to my man.

Thank you to my man, thank you to my man.

THE END

Did you enjoy the read?
Let us know how much by leaving us a review on Amazon
and Goodreads.

PREVIEW

Keep reading for a preview of…

Trickin' On A Heaux For Christmas

By Telia Teanna

CHAPTER 1

"You really not about to come spend Christmas with us this year, my nigga?" DaQuan's best friend, Reggie, asked in disappointment.

DaQuan "Day" Mitchell sighed heavily and shook his head at his friend. "Nah, man…"

Reginal White was Day's OG, a man that was nine years his senior and had taken a young DaQuan under his wing and did his best to give the young man some wisdom and knowledge. Having both been to prison, that was where they met and had maintained a friendship that had extended past the time that they did together behind the wall.

Reggie scoffed at his friend, his face twisting up in disbelief. He was well aware of the fact that if Day rejected his invitation to spend the holidays with he and his family, then he would be all alone. That was the last thing that he wanted for his boy. He looked at Day as if he was his own son. He had a lot of love for the man and a lot of what he had been through in his tragic life. Being alone during the Christmas season was something that Reggie knew Day didn't need at all. He considered DaQuan family.

"You ain't even got a lil hoe you can ride wit'?" Reggie pursed his lips as he looked disapprovingly at his stubborn friend. Whenever the nigga got in his feelings, he always became difficult to deal with.

"I'm *damn* sure ain't doin' that." Day sucked his teeth. He couldn't imagine spending a couple of hours let alone days with any of the bitches that he found himself sticking his dick in over the last year. They were cool, just not cool enough for him to want to spend Christmas being interrogated by bitches' families. *Hard pass.*

"Maaan… Don't tell me you about to spend the next few days by yourself for no reason… I thought we had a good time last year…"

Day sighed again. The two men were riding around town, doing some Christmas shopping together.

Reggie was a newly married man, and it was the first Christmas that he and his wife, Blessing, would be spending together in addition to his three children, Jr., Lashay, and Maurice. He had put in a lot of overtime and worked on twice as many cars for his auto mechanic shop to make sure that he could give his family a great Christmas. He was a man that worked hard to provide for and take care of his family.

He did it joyously too.

Day shrugged. "It is what it is, bro," he said when he came to a stop at a stop light. He leaned slightly to the left, looking out of his window and taking in the dark purple Sacramento sky. It had just gotten dark, and the grey clouds that stuck out against the plum-colored sky told him that it would be raining soon. He also smelled it in the air when he had stepped outside his apartment. Earlier in the day, it had sprinkled, so the roads were already slightly wet, and the five o'clock traffic was starting to pick up.

We should make it inside by the time it starts to rain, he thought to himself as he put his foot on the gas once the light turned green. DaQuan loved the rain and chilly weather seasons; he just didn't like being *in* them.

They were a few minutes from Westfield Galleria, a mall in Roseville. The two men were quiet the remainder of the ride. After finding a parking spot in the crowded mall, Reggie spoke after unbuckling his seat belt. "Look… we love you, Day. You know you're always welcome, and you'll always have a home with us. You gonna have gifts under that tree from all of us too… Don't ruin my babies' Christmas, bruh." The older man stepped out of Day's black Lincoln Navigator.

Day sat there for a moment, considering what his friend had said to him, and a slight smile tugged at the corner of his lips. It felt good to know that he had *someone* who had love for him. After gathering his thoughts, he stepped out of his car and into the chilled air. The man inhaled deeply, taking the cold winter air into his lungs. A strong gust of wind blowing caused him to pull his black beanie down over his ears and the collar of his black pea coat up over the back of his neck.

"Whew! It's gettin' cold as a muthafucka out here. That

damn wind just made my nuts shrivel up!" Reggie cursed, rubbing his gloved hands together.

Day laughed, and they both started jogging through the parking lot and into the busy mall. It started to pour down raining as soon as they made it inside.

"Everybody and they mama in here tonight," Reggie said, mugging a man that had bumped into him on their way inside of a Shoe Palace store. "Excuse you, nigga!"

"Chill. There's only a few more days until Christmas. Everybody doin' they last minute shopping." Day pointed out, his eyes scanning the wall of name brand shoes on display. Some new age rapper was blasting through the speakers of the store. The song was catchy, something that he was sure would be annoyingly on repeat in his head. "People making money and spending money non-stop 'til it gets here."

"Can I help you fine gentlemen with anything?" A sweet and seductive voice met the men's ears.

Both of the men turned to face the owner of the voice and looked down at the tiny woman standing before them. A young woman with a pretty golden complexion, who was no more than nineteen years old, was standing with her hands behind her back, bouncing on her tiptoes. Her black hair was slicked back into a long and straight ponytail that cascaded down her back. A big grin was on her face, exposing the set of red braces in her mouth. The nametag pinned to her shirt read "Kelsie."

Kelsie had been eyeing the two men since she saw them walking into the store. One of them was tall, standing at about six feet tall, and wore a black pea coat, dark washed jeans, and a pack of black Air Forces. She found him to be extremely attractive with his chocolate skin, full salt and pepper sprinkled beard, and deep-set brown eyes. He was hella fine, and there was something about his presence that held weight. She wasn't sure what it was, but it was exactly what had her standing in front of them, cheesing and batting her dramatic false eyelashes.

Ew... Day thought to himself, turned off by her overly dramatic attempt at flirting. *Thirsty ass...*

The young woman's eyes turned to Reggie and took in his five-foot-eight height and big round belly. He was dressed a lot similar to his friend, but instead, he wore black work boots on his feet. The man was obviously a lot older, thanks to the grey stubble growing on his face and the heavy look of exhaustion on his face. He was a decent looking man, but he wasn't her focus. His boy was.

"Nah, we good, miss," Day said flatly and turned his back to the woman and went back to looking at the shoes on the wall.

"Thank you, sweetheart, but we're good for now. We'll give you a call if we need anything." Reggie let the young girl down easy when he saw her face fall after being rejected by Day. That nigga had a cold way of acting sometimes. "Damn, nigga, you ain't have to do that lil girl like that." He chuckled at his friend. "Yo ass gon' be single forever wit that attitude." He picked up a colorful women's sneaker and began to examine it.

Day rolled his eyes and ignored his friend. Irritation was

beginning to fill him; he really didn't want to be out and about shopping, and he *really* didn't want to talk about his lack of a serious relationship. His love life was always a touchy subject for him. He didn't like dwelling in the mental space of love and intimacy. The sound of his phone dinging and the vibration against his leg caught his attention, and he pulled it out of his pocket.

A small smile tugged at his lips when he saw the contact bubble with the letter "J" in it. When he opened the message, it read:

J: I swear you are too sweet to me. My day was a little hectic… but other than that… eh, my day was okay. How was yours?

Day had been anxiously waiting for the message all day. She had taken longer to reply than usual. He was relieved that he had received one at all.

D: I could never be sweeter than you though, Mz Juicyy… My day was okay too.

D: Okay days are still good ones. Work was crazy?

After he slipped his phone back into his pocket, he grabbed a pair of boy cleats that he thought that Jr., Reggie's oldest son, would like. The fourteen-year-old had started high school and was on the football team. A new pair of athletic shoes for the sport was something that the teen had made clear that he wanted for the upcoming holiday. It was on the list that he had pasted to the window of his Navigator one day after visiting the family a couple of weeks prior.

DaQuan hadn't noticed it but receiving the text from Juicyy had eased his irritation. "You think Jr. would like these?" he asked, holding up a green and black pair that matched the colors of his high school's team.

"Yeah, he'll fuck with 'em… as long as you're there to give 'em to 'im." The older man shrugged. He was trolling him, but he didn't care as long as it helped him achieve his goal.

Day sighed. "Aye, man… why you gotta be like that? I get y'all want me to be there… but real shit, my nigga… when I'm around y'all… especially since you and Bless got married…" He shook his head and took a seat on a bench. He looked around for Kelsie and held the cleat in the air along with eight fingers, signaling the size that he needed.

Kelsie was watching him from afar and nodded in response to his request before disappearing into the back. Day turned his attention back to Reggie.

"It just make a nigga realize I'm lonely…"

Reggie was at a loss for words, and his heart went out to his friend. He could only imagine what it could possibly feel like to be in a room full of people that he knew loved him yet still feel alone.

Day had no wife, no kids, no parents, or any siblings. Most of his childhood, he jumped from foster home to foster home until he aged out of the system and began running the streets. He never had a family until he met Reginald, and that was something that he thanked God for daily. If it hadn't been for Reggie, DaQuan was sure that he would have crashed out a long time ago.

Reggie didn't know what to say, so he didn't say anything at all. They sat quietly and waited for Kelsie to come out with the cleats.

DaQuan blew out a fast breath as he closed the front door of his one-bedroom apartment and locked it for the night. The man pressed his forehead to the door in exhaustion, taking a few moments to gather himself before moving away from the front door. Being out and about in public always drained him.

After recuperating some of his strength, he made his way to his bedroom where he began stripping out of his clothes so that he could prepare to get in the shower. His phone dinging again caught his attention. He was in nothing but his underwear when he picked his jeans up from the floor and pulled his phone from the pocket to respond to Juicyy's message.

J: You're right. Okay days are still good ones. I needed that reminder. Work, on the other hand, was something else but nothing I couldn't handle.

Day frowned. He didn't like the sound of that.

D: I'm gonna take a shower, and when I get out, I'ma call you, and we can talk about it, aight?

Once he sent the message, he sent her an Apple Cash payment of $100 to secure his time with her. He wasn't going to give her an opportunity to tell him no. Juicyy had a bad habit of doing so every opportunity that she could.

He had learned long ago how to deal with the stubborn woman.

J: Okay...

Her response came soon after he sent the money, and he smirked in satisfaction. He was a man that liked control and loved it when he got his way.

When he was sure that she'd be answering his call after he showered, he put on his favorite playlist and let the sounds of T.I.'s *Why You Wanna* echo off the bathroom walls as he showered. Juicyy was on his mind, and his dick hardened in anticipation of talking to the sexy woman.

Day had come across her on Twitter years prior while behind the wall. He had developed quite the affinity for porn, and while scrolling through the dark depths of the social media platform, he came across Mz Juicyy.

The woman was a plus sized, bronze skinned beauty who was confident in herself, her sexuality, and her body. Sitting at two hundred sixty pounds, she carried most of her weight in her large breasts and her wide hips. A mental image of one of his favorite pictures of her was etched into his head, making pre-cum drip from the head of his dick as he slowly washed his body and enjoyed the warm water that heated the bathroom as he showered. The mental visual of the pear shape of her ass was etched behind his eyelids. While it wasn't completely rounded, it was wider and flatter near the top but rounded out nicely at the bottom of her cheeks. He loved to watch her bounce and shake her ass from different angles on her Twitter page.

She was thick as hell, knew her body, how to dress it and all the angles in a way that made men all over the world lust after her. She knew just what to do to have her followers eating out of the palms of her tiny hands.

Not to mention that she had the sexiest voice that he had ever heard. It was often that Day would scroll through her Twitter page in the mornings and listen to the erotic voice messages that she recorded of herself telling erotic stories while masturbating to start his days off on the right note. There were many audiences, fetishes, and kinks that she catered to. She had a special way of capitalizing off of her wildly sensual and erotic nature and talents.

He loved that shit.

For a year, Day watched her page and content, learning all that he could about her based on the tweets that she made, the content she shared, and how she interacted with others. It was after she had disappeared for some months that he reached out to her via direct message, asking if she was okay and that he hoped that she had been doing well. He was pleasantly surprised when she had replied and let him know that life had been difficult, and she just needed a break.

That had been the beginning of one of the most meaningful connections in his life. For so long, he had watched her from afar, wishing that he could get to know her on a deeper, more personal level and get to know the woman *behind* the camera and content. When he got the opportunity to get to know her on a more personal level, he couldn't help the attraction that he had to the unique woman.

Nearly four years later and the two were the best of friends and had a relationship that was just as unique as they both were. Their connection was undeniable, and the sexual tension between them was through the roof. Day had been patient with her. It had been one thing when he was locked up, but it was a whole different thing now that he was free.

I shoulda been had that pussy, he thought to himself, thoroughly annoyed. *She know good and damn well she feelin' a nigga… but won't even let me see her face. She got me fucked up.*

That was the catch when it came to Mz Juicyy. Though she shared her body to the world, she had yet to show that face of hers. Even after becoming special friends with benefits with her, she still refused to show him her face. Granted, he didn't share his with her either, but at that point in their relationship, he felt like their face reveals were long overdue.

Something that Day knew but refused to accept was the fact that she didn't trust him enough for her to be that vulnerable with him.

It hurt him that he felt ready to take that step but having to wait on her for so long made him feel some type of way. He was ready to move forward with their connection, and her hesitance frustrated him to no end.

I want her! What the fuck is so hard for her to understand about that? After washing his body with a white washcloth, he stepped under the showerhead and allowed the hot water to cascade down over his body and relax his tense muscles. *Yeah… I know how I'll handle this.*

After finishing his shower, Day stepped out, completely dried his body with a black towel, and then walked butt ass naked to his bedroom where he crawled in and got comfortable. His dick was still on brick when he picked up his cell phone and called Juicyy after plugging his AirPods into his ears.

"Hello?" The velvety voice on the other end of the phone immediately made the head of his dick swell with lust.

"Ready to tell me about work?" He adjusted himself in the

bed so that he was lying on his back with one hand on his stomach, the other behind his head. His body relaxed into the bed the moment he heard her voice. It had been a couple of days since he last talked to her. He missed her voice.

She chuckled. "Not really… It wasn't nothing major. Just had a crazy ass client… That's all."

"He hurt you?" He needed to know.

"Nah… he tried it though… until I pulled that thang on his ass." She giggled giddily.

Day didn't laugh. "I don't like that shit, Juice…"

A heavy sigh met his ears. "I know… I don't either."

They were both quiet for a few minutes, lost in their own thoughts.

DaQuan didn't know what to say. On one hand, he wanted to be able to solve all of her problems, something that he could easily do, but again, he had learned that he couldn't push too hard with Juicyy, or she would go running. He was tired of chasing her fine ass. He wanted her to willingly give herself to him.

Mz Juicyy had him doing everything he swore he would never do to get a woman. DaQuan was far from a trick, but he had no problems tricking on Juicyy. If anything, the fact that she *could* get him to trick on her turned him on even more.

His dick throbbed at the realization.

"What you want for Christmas this year?" he asked, breaking their silence.

"Hmm…" She thought for a moment. "Honestly, I don't know. Nothing comes to mind at the moment."

He imagined that she was shrugging and rolled his eyes. Typical answer for her. "Know what I want?"

"What's that?"

His dick throbbed again. "You."

Silence.

"Juice…"

"Hmm?"

"Come spend Christmas with me."

"D…" It came out as a whine.

"I don't wanna hear shit but a yes. I'm tired of hearing you tell me no. We ain't doing that shit no more. That's over wit'." His mind had been made up.

"How you go–"

"I said I don't wanna hear shit but a yes. Where am I booking your flight from? You still in Vegas?" Day sat up, grabbed his laptop from the nightstand to the right of his bed, opened it, and pulled up an airline website. "What you wanna fly? Southwest?"

He heard her suck her teeth and smirked. He loved irritating her.

"We're not doing this…"

"Why not? I'ma pay yo fee, and I'ma cover yo accommodations. What makes me any different than any of the other niggas you sell pussy to? You gon' be fuckin' that day anyway… Why not come fuck on me? I deserve that shit, don't I?" Day was being extremely direct, something he usually tried not to be with Juicyy's sensitive ass. He waited a few moments for her to respond.

Instead of answering any of those questions, she answered a previous one instead. "Yeah, I'm still in Vegas..."

He rolled his eyes but accepted the answer she gave him. He would get those answers one way or another. "Aight, say less. I'll book yo flight now. Send me your information."

"Damn, I gotta give you my name too? Why can't I book my own flight?" She teased.

"'To ensure yo ass gon' get on that muthafucka. I know you won't make me waste my money," he said as he scrolled through flights. "You tired?"

Another heavy sigh met his ears. He didn't care. He was getting his way. "Mmm, not really. I'm off a Red Bull. I ain't goin' to sleep no time soon."

"Perfect. I'ma put you on this 7:20 a.m. flight then. Name."

"Woah, woah, woah... *woah*... That's only a few hours from now!" She sounded almost panicked.

"I know... What's the problem?" Day was annoyed by her hesitance.

"That doesn't leave me any time to pack or nothin'," she said as if she was pointing out the obvious.

"Okay, and? You don't need anything. Anything you'll need, I'll provide for you." He replied back as if it was that simple. They were though when fucking with him.

"Is that right?" Her voice dropped a few octaves.

"Damn right. Name." He demanded again.

"Ticy Jones. 11/17/1994." She gave in, giving him her name and birthdate.

The grin that spread across Day's face when she had

finally given him her government almost split his face. For years, he had done his best to find out anything he could about her identity, but she was good at protecting herself. Now that he had a name *and* a birthday... There was nothing in the way of keeping him from finding and pulling up on her when he pleased.

"T.I.C.Y.?"

"Mhmm..."

Day spent a few minutes securing the early morning fight. "Okay... booked. I'm sending you the boarding pass now."

"How long you keeping me?" He could hear the sound of a zipper in the background. He assumed it was some kind of luggage that she was getting ready to pack. He bit his bottom lip, his mind running with excitement. *This is really about to happen.* He had been fantasizing about the day that they would meet for a long time.

DaQuan couldn't wait.

"To keep it a hunnit wit' you, Juice... I don't plan on ever letting you go..."

"Ummm... that sounds like kidnapping, sir..."

He chuckled darkly. "If that's what you wanna call it..." He reached a hand down and gripped the base of his throbbing dick. A man of dark desires, the thought further excited him.

Juicyy was quiet on the other side of the phone. She knew what was up. She knew him enough to know what he was *really* saying.

"You something else, you know that?" She chuckled.

"Mhm, just make sure yo ass on that flight... Don't make

me come find you, *Ticy*." He liked the way her name rolled off his tongue.

"Yeah…" She paused. "I hear you… You better not be ugly." She giggled.

Day laughed. "*You* better not be ugly, girl."

"Stop playin' with me. You know I'm big fine."

"Oou, I fuckin' know it. You need to stop playin' wit' *me* and come get this money. Let me spoil you for the holidays. You ain't got nobody, and I don't have a family of my own… Why not spend it together? You ain't gotta be alone, Juice." He paused momentarily to catch up his thoughts. "And real shit… I don't wanna be alone either. A nigga tired of being lonely… I know you are too."

DaQuan was surprised by his level of transparency in that moment. He allowed himself to speak on his true feelings, and that was a scary thing, but it was also exactly what he knew he needed.

Day was positive that once they got in one another's presence, neither of them would want to go back to just being sexting buddies again. He just needed the opportunity to show her differently.

Their time was about to arrive.

"I can't say that you're wrong… but I can say that I'm scared, D."

His stomach dropped at the heavy emotion that he could hear in her voice when she spoke. "I would never hurt you, baby."

"I don't think that you would. At least not intentionally… I'm scared because… I think I'm falling for you…"

His heart nearly skipped a beat. "Fall, baby... fall. I promise I'll catch you."

You've got this, girl. It's just another meetup... but with D... Ticy thought, giving herself a pep talk to calm her nerves.

D: Let me know when you board.

She was sitting in her designated terminal, waiting to board her flight, when his text came through and made her smile. *I'm really about to meet this nigga...*

It had been a long time coming, and the thudding of her clit against the seat of her panties mimicked the quick thudding of her heart. It had been a long four years and having talked every day since D had reached out to her, their physical union had been long overdue. At the start of their relationship, D had been in prison and was communicating with her via a cell phone that he had somehow gotten his hands on.

What started out as him checking on her after an extended hiatus turned into him becoming a regular client of hers who purchased adult content and phone sex sessions from her. Originally, it had been all about what *she* could do for *him*, but as time went on, it became about what they could do for *each other.*

J: Will do. Boarding now, waiting on my group to be called.

Ticy responded to D's message then put her phone in the pocket of her sweater. She was wearing a white Juicy Couture tracksuit with a white tank top under the hoodie that she was gifted from one of her tricks. It was one of her favorite outfits and hugged her size sixteen frame perfectly. Since she was on the shorter side, she had to get the pants hemmed to accommodate her height, and a pair of Steve Madden wedges on her little feet gave her a couple of more inches. She knew that she would need them.

When her boarding group was called, Ticy stood up, slung her purse over her shoulder, and was grabbing the handle of her carry-on suitcase and getting in line to get on the plane when a thought struck her. She pulled her phone out of her pocket to send another quick text.

J: You're picking me up, right?

D: Of course I am.

J: How am I gonna know who you are?

D: You'll know ;)

Ticy chuckled at the message and shook her head as she tucked her phone back into her pocket. The young woman's mind was reeling with thoughts of D, and she mentally prepared herself for an experience that she knew that she would never forget.

Ten minutes later, Ticy was in her seat, looking out the window, butterflies filling her stomach. Right before she was about to put her phone on airplane mode, she got another text. When she opened it, it was another Apple Cash payment from D.

$5,500.

A smile pulled at her glossy lips, and her panties dampened even more. Nothing made her wetter than receiving some money.

Yeah, we're gonna have a good ass time. Fuck it…

Ticy had a lot of anxiety about meeting D for many different reasons. Due to the nature of her job, she had a rule to never get too personal with her clients to the point that she found herself catching feelings for any of them. It was difficult to capture the woman's interest let alone keep it. But someway, somehow, D, a man who hadn't even given her his name yet, had managed to get hers and get her ass on a flight to spend Christmas with him.

I'll give him a week… Maybe once we finally have sex, all these feelings will go away. Logically, she knew that it didn't make any sense, but that was all she could do at that point.

The flight was only an hour and a half, so Ticy spent it listening to a playlist that D had made for her and allowed herself to daydream and fantasize about what she would do when they finally came face to face. *Will he kiss me? What if he really is ugly? I'll be so damn disappointed.* She shook her head at the tragic thought.

Before she knew it, the plane was landing, and excitement and anxiety filled her at the same time. She was sitting in the middle of the plane, so she remained seated and waited until it was her turn to be let out of her seat, grab her carry-ons, and exit the plane.

She pulled her phone out of her pocket again and sent a text to D once she was walking through the airport.

J: Just got off the plane…

Ticy was making her way to the baggage claim area when she looked up from her phone and locked eyes with who she *knew* had to be D.

He was a tall man in a white tracksuit, a white fitted hat, white Air Forces on his feet, and a bouquet of purple roses so big that they looked like they would be almost too heavy for her to carry. Ticy found the full salt and pepper beard on his face extremely attractive, and it immediately made her wonder if it was because of genetics that made him grey early or if it was from stress. Either way, she found it to be very sexy. She liked the old man look.

She nearly felt herself blush under his gaze when heat lit up his eyes as he took her in. Her nipples tightened when she saw the tip of his pink tongue swipe across his full bottom lip and then bit down on it while shaking his head as his eyes trailed down her body. Ticy smirked when she realized that he was going to make her walk all the way to him instead of meeting her halfway.

"Mmm, mmm, mmm… I knew yo ass was gonna be fine, but I didn't think you was gonna be *this* fine," Day said and licked his lips again when she made it over to him.

Ticy laughed, the sound coming out a little breathless. The feeling was definitely mutual.

The two were standing less than a foot away when Day stretched a hand out and grabbed her by the hem of her sweater and firmly pulled her into him so that the front of her body was pressed flush against his. Ticy stopped breathing momentarily, his action and the aggressiveness of it catching her off guard. That was until he leaned down and took her lips, passionately kissing her.

"Mmm…" She moaned into his mouth when he slipped his tongue between her lips, deepening the kiss. Her kitty began to purr when Day reached down and squeezed a handful of her ass with his free hand and used it to pull her into him even closer. Ticy groaned and resisted the urge to slip a hand between them to caress the bulge she felt growing against her stomach.

Making out in the middle of the airport was something Ticy normally avoided. Public displays of affection were a no go in her world, well unless a nigga *paid* her to do so, but even then she had boundaries.

But with D, all that shit went out of the window.

He pulled away from her and slapped her on her juicy booty and then handed her the large bouquet of flowers. "Ain't wanna show up empty handed, and I know you like flowers and shit, so here you go." A half smile pulled at the left side of his face when Ticy nearly toppled over from the big ass bouquet.

She was flattered that he had remembered that small tidbit about her. Being that she basically lived out of hotels, thanks to her choice in occupation, flowers were something that she bought on a regular basis to bring good energy and beauty into the rooms to help lift her usually down spirits. The purple color was perfect.

Ticy smiled, sniffing the sweet smelling flowers, and looked up at the thoughtful gift. *I don't know where we gonna find a vase big enough to hold them up, but we'll figure it out.* She was happy and appreciative of the gift. "You wanna give me your name now? That way I can thank you properly."

"Day," he simply replied.

"Thank you, Day."

He nodded.

Day grabbed the handle of her carryon and turned to the conveyor belt where all the travelers' luggage circled.

"That one." Ticy pointed to a rose gold colored suitcase that was a larger version of her carryon.

Effortlessly, he grabbed it as it moved past him and pulled the heavy bag off the belt. "Damn, seems like you had more than enough time to pack," he said as they began walking through the airport and to the exit.

"Why don't you ever buy me flowers?" The pair heard a female voice scream followed by a loud slapping noise.

"See, ya ass always worried about the wrong shit. Now look at ya! Cryin' and lookin' stupid for tryna embarrass me in public." A man's voice shouted.

Day and Ticy looked at one another as they walked and then shook their heads in sync, making them burst out laughing.

"Look what you started." Ticy teased, playfulness evident in her voice.

Day grinned. "Shiiit…" he replied dismissively.

The two were quiet as they walked through the airport, the big bouquet of flowers attracting many stares, compliments, whispers, and envious gazes. When they made it to the parking lot, Ticy trailed slightly behind Day, allowing him to lead the way to his car.

When they were close, Day hit the button on his car to unlock the doors and alert Ticy to which vehicle was his. Ticy's eyebrows rose upon seeing the "Lincoln" emblem on the back of the truck. She slightly nodded her head in approval as she mentally began adding up numbers.

He sent me a hunnit last night… $5,500 when I got on the plane… These damn roses were at least a couple hunnit dollars… and he has a Lincoln… He's definitely sittin' on some paper.

Ticy knew that Day had money; he never hesitated to pay her prices for the kind of custom content that he wanted from her, some of it being far from what she would call "cheap." But her relationship with him was different than it was with all her other clients. It wasn't until she was climbing into the leather seat of the car that she realized that after all the time that they had been talking, she hadn't been clocking his pockets. Being the hoe that she was, she was a professional pocket watcher. Always aware of what others around her had to offer.

"Thank you." Her voice was low and seductive as Day leaned over her to put her seatbelt on for her. She knew that he was just using that as an opportunity to touch on her when his hand brushed across her G-cups.

She let him, taking that time to inhale his scent. Immediately, her head began to swim with lust. There was something about scents that always got her going.

Right when Day was withdrawing from leaning over, Ticy gently put three manicured fingers under his chin, making him look at her. They stared into each other's eyes, silently communicating. Then, she leaned in and kissed him again. This time, it was slow, sweet, sensual, and passionate.

The young woman could feel a buzzing in her lips, almost as if there was an electrical current running through them.

She had never felt anything like it before! A minute later, Day pulled away, and it wasn't until she had opened her eyes that she realized they had drifted closed in the middle of the kiss. Somehow, she had gotten lost in it. He was staring intensely at her, taking in her pretty face.

"Let me hurry up and get yo fine ass to this room so I can tear yo juicy ass up," he said, his voice low and deep.

"Yeah, you do that," Ticy replied seductively and then bit her lip.

Day stood up straight and smirked, closed the passenger side door before loading her luggage into the trunk, and then got into the driver seat.

"Ready to have the best Christmas ever, Mz Juicyy?" Day asked as he backed out of the parking space then looked at her.

"Best Christmas ever, huh? I suppose so." She giggled, looking back at him.

"Just watch and see, baby. Watch and see."

Available Now

On all online retail book platforms!

ALSO BY P. WISE

My Curves Captivated a Hood Millionaire: A BBW Love Story

My Curves Captivated a Hood Millionaire: A BBW Love Story 2

Come Play In It: An Urban Erotica

Heir to the Plug's Throne

Heir to the Plug's Throne 2

Gorgeous Gangstas

Gorgeous Gangstas 2

Gorgeous Gangstas 3

Luchiano Mob Ties: Snatched Up by a Don Spin-Off

Snatched Up by a Don: A BBW Love Story

Snatched Up by a Don: A BBW Love Story 2

Snatched Up by a Don: A BBW Love Story 3

A Saint Luv'n A Savage: A Philly Love Story

Luv'n a Philly Boss: A Saint Luv'n a Savage Spin-off

Kwon: Clone of a Savage

Kwon: Clone of a Savage 2

Welcome to Cherrieville: Bitter & Sweet

Summer Luvin' with a NY Baller

Tamia & Tytus: A Toxic Love Affair

Diary of a Brooklyn Girl

Sex, Scams, & Brisks

Sex, Scams, & Brisks 2

OTHER BOOKS BY

<u>URBAN AINT DEAD</u>

Tales 4rm Da Dale

The Hottest Summer Ever

By **Elijah R. Freeman**

Despite The Odds

By **Juhnell Morgan**

Good Girl Gone Rogue

By **Manny Black**

Hittaz

Hittaz 2

Hittaz 3

Coldhearted

By **Lou Garden Price, Sr.**

Charge It To The Game

Charge It To The Game 2

A Summer To Remember With My Hitta

Snatched Up By A Hitta

By **Nai**

A Setup For Revenge

By **Ashley Williams**

Ridin' For You

By **Telia Teanna**

The State's Witness

The State's Witness 2

By **Kyiris Ashley**

Stuck In The Trenches

Stuck In The Trenches 2

By **Huff Tha Great**

The Swipe

By **Toōla**

BOOKS BY

URBAN AINT DEAD's C.E.O

<u>Elijah R. Freeman</u>

Triggadale

Triggadale 2

Triggadale 3

Tales 4rm Da Dale

The Hottest Summer Ever

Murda Was The Case

Murda Was The Case 2

Murda Was The Case 3

STAY CONNECTED

Follow
Elijah R. Freeman
On Social Media
FB: Elijah R. Freeman
IG: @the_future_of_urban_fiction

www.ingramcontent.com/pod-product-compliance
Lightning Source LLC
Chambersburg PA
CBHW070654010826
48975CB00013B/1173